P9-CSG-626

For more than forty years,
Yearling has been the leading name
in classic and award-winning literature
for young readers.

Yearling books feature children's
favorite authors and characters,
providing dynamic stories of adventure,
humor, history, mystery, and fantasy.

Trust Yearling paperbacks to entertain,
inspire, and promote the love of reading
in all children.

OTHER YEARLING BOOKS YOU WILL ENJOY

WORLD OF ADVENTURE OMNIBUS, *Gary Paulsen*

THE TRAP, *Joan Lowery Nixon*

THE SWISS FAMILY ROBINSON, *Johann Wyss*

SMILE!, *Geraldine McCaughrean*

THE SIGN OF THE BEAVER, *Elizabeth George Speare*

THE MYSTERY OF HERMIT DAN, *Peggy Parish*

FROZEN STIFF, *Sherry Shahan*

FISH, *L. S. Matthews*

LEEPIKE RIDGE

N. D. WILSON

A YEARLING BOOK

Copyright © 2007 by N. D. Wilson

All rights reserved. No part of this book may be reproduced or transmitted in any
form or by any means, electronic or mechanical, including photocopying, recording,
or by any information storage and retrieval system, without the written permission
of the publisher, except where permitted by law. For information address
Random House Books for Young Readers.

Yearling and the jumping horse design are registered trademarks
of Random House, Inc.

Visit us on the Web! www.randomhouse.com/kids
Educators and librarians, for a variety of teaching tools,
visit us at www.randomhouse.com/teachers

The Library of Congress has cataloged the hardcover edition of this work as follows:
Wilson, N. D.   Leepike Ridge / N. D. Wilson   p. cm.
Summary: While his widowed mother continues to search for him, eleven-year-old
Tom, presumed dead after slipping underground while drifting down a river, finds
himself trapped in a series of underground caves with another survivor and a dog,
and pursued by murderous treasure-hunters.
ISBN: 978-0-375-83873-6 (trade)—ISBN: 978-0-375-93873-3 (lib. bdg.)
[1. Missing persons—Fiction. 2. Caves—Fiction. 3. Adventure and adventurers—
Fiction. 4. Mothers and sons—Fiction. 5. Buried treasure—Fiction.] I. Title.
PZ7.W69744Lee 2007   [Fic]—dc22   2006013352
ISBN: 978-0-375-83874-3 (pbk.)

Reprinted by arrangement with Random House Books for Young Readers
Printed in the United States of America
July 2008
10 9 8 7 6 5 4 3 2
First Yearling Edition

For my boys and my beauties

CONTENTS

LEEPIKE RIDGE

~ one ~

TIME
(ONCE UPON A)

In the history of the world there have been lots of *onces* and lots of *times*, and every time has had a once upon it. Most people will tell you that the once upon a time happened in a land far, far away, but it really depends on where you are. The once upon a time may have been just outside your back door. It may have been beneath your very feet. It might not have been in a land at all but deep in the sea's belly or bobbing around on its back.

In this case it was in a land, for the most part. If you know of a valley where a small mountain peak once shaped like a crescent moon has tumbled down and disturbed the old willow trees growing beside a slow stream, then this story does not begin far, far away, and you've probably already heard it. But if you, like me, had to be told about this valley and the stream and the old, dry house chained to the top of the enormous rock beside the foot of the mountain, then this story does begin once upon a time in a land most definitely far, far away. Anyone close to this valley is sure to have heard of it.

Our story had already begun when the dust-covered delivery truck found the gravel road leading into the valley and followed it to its end beside the old willow rock. Two men got out and glared at the wooden stairs that crawled up to the house.

"Don't know what sort of people would build up there," the driver muttered.

"People who liked rocks, maybe. Or views."

"Or stairs."

Thomas Hammond, who was down by the stream with a red plastic cup full of leeches, heard them and turned to watch. They fished the large refrigerator box out of the back of the truck and strapped thick belts beneath thicker bellies, preparing to tote it to the top, two more deliverymen in a long history of delivery-men who would sweat and curse their way up the long, curving stairs. Finally, at the top, his mother greeted them and held the kitchen door open as they squeezed the box inside.

Tom had traveled around the sun eleven times when the delivery truck brought his mother's newest fridge, but a number doesn't really describe his age. His father had been gone for three years, and that made him feel older. He was the sort of boy who had many friends when he was at school, but what they knew about him was limited to his freckles, brown hair, long arms, and the clenched determination that settled onto his face when he was angry or competing. His smile, which was wide and quick, was always surprising, and his laugh, which lived in his narrow belly, was unpredictable. In games, any games, he was the first to dive for a ball, to slide on concrete, or to get a mouthful of dirt. He was taller than many of the boys in his class, but not the tallest, and he always seemed to have scabs.

Wait for the rest of the story, and you will know him better when I am done.

People thought Tom's house was chained to the top of the rock for a reason. Some said the first house in the valley had been built down by the stream and that the spring floods had washed it away. The second house, they said, had been built on top of the rock, but one of the big summer thunderstorms had blown it off. So the third house had been chained to spikes bored deep into the stone. But no one really knew why or when the house had been built, only that it was there now and it had stayed put through lifetimes, though occasional electrical surges were hard on lightbulbs and appliances. The lightbulbs were easy to replace and the appliances were usually under warranty, so Tom's mother, Elizabeth, didn't mind. She didn't have to carry the new ones up the stairs.

When the truck had gone and the dust had settled, Tom dumped forty-seven confused leeches onto the bank, where he thought the birds would find them and be pleasantly surprised. Cup in hand, he jumped through the long grass and ran up the stairs to look at his mother's shiny new refrigeration. At the top he found the box. It was lying on its side, carefully arranged and waiting for him. He bent over and looked in. A long brick of white foam filled the bottom, and a small stack of cookies sat on it, all the way at the end. Why? Tom wondered. Why does she think I still want to play in boxes?

Tom got down on his knees and retrieved the cookies. Back on his feet, he ate thoughtfully as he kicked at the fridge box and watched it skid across the rock. He kicked again, and the box tumbled down the rock and out onto the breeze. Tom watched plastic packing bags slip out, followed by the large piece of foam. The box bounced in the gravel drive and rolled into the long grass, but the foam floated nicely, clearing the first willow trees. The plastic bags disappeared.

"Hey!" his mother called from inside. "You'd better

get that all picked up before some duck chokes on it! Come in and see the fridge!"

"We don't have ducks," Tom said. He stared at the last cookie in his hand, counted the chocolate chips, and then slid the whole thing into his mouth.

It was a nice fridge, too big for the corner of the kitchen where it would live out its electrically dangerous life. It was black and shiny, in sharp contrast to the dingy kitchen, and it had water and ice in the door. The last two fridges had both had the water and ice dispensers in the door but had never dispensed either one. They wouldn't work without a water line, and a water line had never been run.

"Well, you can head back out," Elizabeth said when the tour was over. "Try not to be too long, though. Jeffrey is coming to dinner, and I'll need help setting." She gave him half of a wide smile. "And see if you can track down all that trash you just spread through the valley."

She pushed her blond hair behind her ears and turned back to the pile of potato peels in the kitchen sink. Tom stood at the door, looking back at his tall, slender mother with her hands full of potato. He usually liked to watch his mother cook, but he didn't like watching her cook for Jeffrey.

Tom found the box easily enough. He danced

around it, picked his spot, and then kicked it back toward the base of the stairs. He liked the sound it made, and he liked how far one kick could send something so big. Searching for the plastic bags and the foam, he crossed the stream on an old fallen log, wandered into the willow trees, and walked from canopy to canopy, pushing his way through the curtains formed by the weeping branches. Occasionally he could see his house, perched on top of the rock, and occasionally the whole world would disappear and he would be left with nothing but the trunk and branches of a willow and a nest full of noisy birds hanging out over the slow water.

It was in one of these willow worlds that he found the foam. It had landed high up in the tree, and never had Tom seen anything that seemed so out of place, unless he counted seeing Jeffrey at his own dining room table, sitting in his father's chair. Tom tried not to think of Jeffrey or the way he smiled at his mother. He tried hard not to be angry with his mother for smiling back. Instead, he focused on finding rocks he could throw at the foam.

When he had collected a small pile, he began to assault the large foam brick from within the tree. Or at least he tried. A vertical throw is difficult enough without a tangled canopy of branches getting in the way. Tom would lean as far back as his balance would allow, cock his hand low to the earth, and then, starting with his legs and stomach, he would uncoil, bringing his arm around as hard as he could. The rock would rattle in the branches, and Tom would duck and dart around, trying to avoid getting hit, until it returned to the soft earth with a slap or to the muddy water with a plop.

He was on his second pile of rocks, and his shoulder was beginning to ache, when he finally hit the white slab. The rock bounced off a branch on the way back down and hit him on the arm, but Tom didn't mind. The foam slid down the willow branches like a sled. It slowed, then tripped free and spun out into the water.

Nearly an hour passed, and Tom didn't know it. He traveled two hundred yards beside the stream, assaulting the floating foam with clods, rocks, branches, and mud. At times, he approached the water's edge with a slick lump of willow wood and hurled it at the white craft, sending the foam into the reeds with the splash when it fell short. Sometimes he retreated and bombarded the thing from a distance, assigning the foam a variety of villainous passengers, most of whom drowned.

Tom had almost rounded the bend in the valley when he saw the dust trail of what he knew must be Jeffrey's little car. He then noticed the time and the grime on his hands, and he wondered if he'd heard his mother yelling for him a little while before. He couldn't be quite sure.

The foam ended up tucked beneath a willow tree, and Tom, breathing heavily, met Jeffrey at the bottom of the stairs. Tom had every intention of being polite. At least, he wasn't planning on calling the man any names.

"You've been playing hard," Jeffrey said, and reached out to touch Tom's head. Tom ducked and then straightened up slowly, looking Jeffrey in the eye.

"What game was it?" Jeffrey asked.

"Nothing," Tom said, and he stepped around him and hurried up the stairs. His mother met him at the top. She was smiling, but Tom saw her glance at his hands and sweaty hair.

"Wash up," she said. "I called for you."

"Sorry," he murmured.

"Hello, Jeffrey." The cheerfulness in her voice bothered Tom. "You got a haircut!"

"I got 'em all cut," Jeffrey said. But Tom heard nothing else because he shut the kitchen door behind him.

Everyone said Jeffrey was a nice man. He was also tall, with lanky limbs and a saggy middle. Worse than that, he had a saggy chest and wore unbuttoned polo shirts. He always smiled, regardless of the situation, and taught fourth grade at Tom's school. He drove a little green car the color of dry toothpaste. To Tom, he had been Mr. Veatch until this summer, when suddenly he had begun dropping by (from his house near school, about twenty miles away) and wanting to be called Jeffrey. As far as Tom was concerned, having to call him Jeffrey was just one step closer to having to call him Dad.

Over dinner, Jeffrey smiled and nodded. He commented on the potatoes. He said he'd spent his day at the library reading up on local history. He thought the nice weather was due to end and wouldn't last through the rest of the weekend. He had heard storms were on the way for Sunday, Monday at the latest. Then he turned to Tom.

"What have you been up to today?" Jeffrey asked. He was chewing while he talked. I don't even do that, Tom thought. He didn't look up. He was sculpting his potatoes.

"Thomas has been playing with the box from the new refrigerator," his mother answered.

Tom's head snapped up, and he felt his teeth squeak.

"Was he, Elizabeth?" Jeffrey asked. "Was he? Oh, I remember those years. One time, I managed to convince my parents to let me save a box from one of our moves—we were always moving—and I took all sorts of things in there and had them all arranged like I was selling them. I must have played store in that box for a week before it finally collapsed after a rain."

Tom was incredulous. This man was admitting to having played store in a box for nearly a week. Tom stared at Jeffrey's long head with its curly, receding hair and the small flap of skinny-man fat that hung beneath his chin.

"I did all sorts of things with boxes," Jeffrey continued. Now Tom was staring at his lips, two chapped leeches that belonged in a cup or, better yet, on the bank waiting for the birds. Except the birds would probably be too grossed out to touch them.

Jeffrey was still talking. "It's healthy for a young boy to use his imagination. I often think that those childish games are what made me what I am today. I remember using one box for a pet store for all my stuffed animals, and another time I missed school so much over a summer vacation that I played classroom almost every day. But that wasn't actually with a box. I did that with the blankets on my bed."

"Well," Elizabeth said. She put her elbows on the table, her chin in her hands, and smiled. "I think Thomas was playing a cruder game. I sent him to pick up all the trash that had blown off the rock, and he ended up playing war with a piece of Styrofoam in the creek."

"I wasn't playing war," Tom said. Still, he thought, it was better than selling stuffed animals out of a box.

"You were throwing things at it."

"I was throwing things at it. I wasn't playing war."

Elizabeth smiled. "I opened the window, and I could hear you making all the same noises you make when you play with your army men."

Tom went red on the outside. Inside, he went black.

"I," he said, and arched his eyebrows into his hair, "do not play with army men."

Jeffrey was laughing. "Oh, you don't need to be embarrassed," he said. "It's natural that a boy your age should still be playing with toys. Even war—though a preoccupation with that particular game could be unhealthy."

Tom stood up.

His mother stopped smiling. "Tom?" she said. A thousand thoughts poured through Tom's head. One hundred things to say. He felt his face relax and his jaw pop, creep forward, and lock. Tom stared at Jeffrey through half-lidded eyes and knew that, just like at school, he wouldn't say anything. Then, to his surprise, his mouth opened.

"Don't ever touch my mother," he said, and he found himself outside. The screen door banged behind him.

Tom stood on the rock and looked around. His

impulse was to go down to the creek and find the piece of packing foam, but that was not an option. He would not be seen with the foam again. He walked to the back corner of the house and stared at the chains that anchored it. Two chains came off the corner, one at the base and the other higher up, near the edge of the roof. Both were attached to the same spike in the rock. After a balancing act, a slip, and some scrambling, Tom was on the roof. A few seconds later he was on the peak, then sitting on the chimney. He did not intend to move until the dust had settled behind Jeffrey Veatch's car, if then.

It didn't take long. Tom sat on the chimney on the house on the enormous rock and overlooked his valley. He stared down at the tops of willow trees and at the stream. He looked at the meadow grass on the other side, and he waited. One solitary mud hen moved in and out of reeds along the water. It isn't a duck, Tom told himself. And it wouldn't try to eat a plastic bag. Then the kitchen door opened, and Tom stopped overlooking and began overlistening.

"Well, Elizabeth," Jeffrey said, "I'll leave you to think over what I've offered."

"You don't need to go because of Tom." She didn't sound happy. Tom thought she sounded like her arms were crossed.

"I want to give him a little space for now. Don't be

too hard on him. It's normal. He doesn't really dislike me. His anger is with himself."

Elizabeth and Jeffrey ended the conversation with pleasantries, and Tom watched Jeffrey's back descend over the edge of the rock. When the little car began spreading its dust trail, Tom's mother spoke.

"Thomas," she said quietly. "You get off the roof right now. You know what I've said about climbing up there."

Tom held his breath and didn't say anything. His mother stepped into view. Her hands were on her hips, and her eyebrows were up. "Do you think I can't hear something your size slipping around on the roof?"

"Did he know?" Tom asked.

"Well, I thought he did," his mother answered. "It was hard not to notice, but I doubt he'd have said what he did if he knew you were listening. You know, Tom, I don't know what makes you do it. Jeffrey likes you."

"He wants to marry you," Tom said.

"I know. He told me."

"What?" Tom caught himself on the chimney. "What did you tell him?"

"Come down, and we'll talk about it."

"I'm not coming down until you tell me what you said."

Elizabeth sighed. "I told him I would think about it. He's coming back tomorrow."

"Why?"

"To hear my answer. Now come down. You should still eat something." Then Elizabeth stepped back inside and shut the door behind her.

When Tom stepped into the house, she was sitting at the table waiting for him, and she had on her determined look. Her fingers were moving, flexing, and drumming on the tabletop. Otherwise, she sat perfectly still.

"Thomas, come sit down."

Tom did.

"Tomorrow," she continued, "you will apologize to Mr. Veatch."

"Jeffrey," Tom said.

"Jeffrey," she said. "Jeffrey wants to try to get to know you better. He wants to play with you down by the creek. You will be polite, and you will look him in the eye when you answer his questions."

"I'll throw up if you marry him," Tom said quietly.

Elizabeth leaned forward. "And I'll have you know something else, Thomas Hammond. I have not decided what I'm going to say to Mr. Veatch tomorrow, but I'm certainly not going to make my decision based on whether or not you are misbehaving."

Eventually, somehow, the evening ended. Dishes were done. The house was tidied. No one was doing much talking. Tom stared at a book for a while. Then he stared at the floor, and then at a couch cushion. At some point his mother kissed him, and when he was lying in bed he knew that he had brushed his teeth because he could taste it, but he couldn't remember doing any actual brushing.

He didn't do any sleeping.

The night was not unusual for the summertime. Tom's window was open, and occasionally a breeze that had stumbled between the two ridges and into the valley would come rolling along, billowing Tom's curtains and rocking the house ever so slightly. Tom listened to the quietly straining chains and felt the house shiver.

He couldn't stop thinking about Jeffrey. He knew that his mother would say no. At least, he knew that she *should* say no. He thought about playing with Jeffrey by the creek. Maybe he would fall in. The piece of foam needed to be gone. There should be no sign that it ever existed. He would sit on the bank and watch Jeffrey get leeches when he waded in the water. If he waded in the water, which he probably wouldn't.

He should get rid of the foam.

Tom pulled on his sneakers without socks and grabbed a sweatshirt from his closet. He knew that his mother would hear the creaks in the hall. They were impossible to get around, so he went to the window. It was not a new route for him, and a moment later he stood on the rock in the warm summer air, pushed by one of the rolling breezes. The moon was up, painting the world silver, making things look just a little more alive.

Tom stared out at the shaggy, moonlit willow heads, and then his feet found the stairs.

~ two ~

VOYAGE

After a few mouthfuls of moon-flavored air, even the stubbornly drowsy can find themselves wide-eyed. Tom was hardly drowsy, and he took more than a few mouthfuls. By the time he had reached the base of the rock, his senses were heightened nearly to the point of bursting. All the normal noises of life were gone, leaving behind the secretive sounds, the shy sounds, the whispers and conversations of moss disputing with grass over some soft piece of earth, or the humming-birds snoring. Tom could hear his toe move in his shoe and willow leaves brushing against each other fifty yards away. He heard a water rat click its teeth, though he hardly knew what it was. He felt as loud as thunder when he walked, so he broke into a run, jumping in the tall grass and pushing his way beneath the weeping willows.

❀   ❀   ❀

Elizabeth was not asleep either. She had heard Tom stirring in his room, but she hadn't heard him in the hall, so she didn't get out of bed. She was thinking. Or at least she was trying to make herself think.

Three years without the husband she loved had begun to wear her down. Tom needed a dad. Jeffrey liked her. Jeffrey even liked Tom. Tom hated Jeffrey.

"Tom can just grow up," she said out loud. She shivered and pulled the blankets up over her head.

Tom had planned on being angry. He'd intended to think dark thoughts out in the night, but the night wouldn't let him. The earth smelled pleasant, and the air, freshly exhaled by the grass and trees, filled his chest. He found the slab of foam under the dark willow belly where he had stored it and tossed it into the water, still beneath the tree.

Willow trees are fond of water, and weeping willows love to dip their fingers. Their branches grow thickest on the waterfront, and they frequently reach the bottom of whatever stream or pond they lean toward.

Tom's foam floated toward the ring of branches draped in the stream and then floated back, too light to push through them. Tom stood and stared at the refrigerator-length piece of foam, and he wondered.

He stopped wondering, and he tested. He put his foot on the foam. Then he squatted down and knelt on it. It still floated. He pushed off the mud bank and drifted toward the leafy ring. He reached out for the branches and quickly dropped onto his belly when the raft rocked and reeled. The leaves parted in front of him as he left his harbor and entered the moonlight.

Tom floated across the stream and pushed off of a large rock. He ran his hands along the bank until he found a stick large enough and began steering himself a course, pushing off of reeds and occasional rocks. His neck grew sore looking up while on his belly, so he got onto his knees but couldn't get comfortable, over-balanced, and nearly fell in. Finally, after a very cautious operation, he managed to lie on his back with his head upstream. His hood was up and his hands were in the pouch of his sweatshirt, though one still gripped his stick. The heels of his shoes skimmed the water's surface.

Tom stared at the stars and the moon and felt as if he'd been awake forever, watching enormous worlds of flame, tiny in the distance, travel through the sky. But then he remembered that *we* are the ones doing the traveling. And that there were as many stars beneath him as there were above. His mind slowed down as he pictured himself floating above an upside-down sky full of stars.

The moon was bright, and as his eyes began to water, he shut them.

The world has seen many men sail down rivers or out to sea lying on rafts or in boats, even on large pyres on the wooden decks of battered warships. These men were usually dead and gripping swords, not sticks, and wearing armor. Sometimes their ships were on fire, and sometimes the men were surrounded by trophies or treasures taken from enemies. Tom was the first one to ever strike such a pose on this stream, though it had been taught the routine by its grandfathers, and it treated him honorably. And while he was definitely the first in history to make such a voyage on white packing foam, being alive when he made it was not terribly original. Plenty of Viking kings had awakened to discover themselves alone on a burning ship with lots of gold. And at least three different men had been roused to consciousness by being dumped over waterfalls, only to drown in the pools below, pulled down by the weight of their armor.

But Tom was still unique, and the water guided him well. He brushed against the reeds but never stopped, and when he came against a rock, the water softened the blow and turned him around to travel headfirst for a while.

Over the years, Tom had followed the stream quite

a ways, well beyond the first curve of the valley. When he had walked beside it, it had always been day, and there had been frogs to catch, small pools to dig, trees to climb, or rocks to roll down the bank into the water. Now, sleeping and carried by the stream's undistracted pace, he traveled much more steadily. And though the stream may have appeared slow, it had always believed that appearances do it an injustice.

Tom made it around the valley's first curve in under an hour, beyond the second in under two, and farther down the stream's course than he had ever traveled in exactly two hours and thirty-seven minutes. He slept soundly. The emotions of the day had drained him, and the initial rousing effect of the night air now soothed his lungs and kept his sleep deep. He dreamt of sailing, and as he dreamt, the valley narrowed, the ridge that led to his own small peak closed in on the stream, and the water quickened.

Tom woke to the sound of human voices and the sensation of falling backward. He was moving fast. The stream had pulled the nose of the foam raft low in the water, and as he jerked awake, it dipped under, spilling water down his back. He was already very cold. The chill of the water, only inches away from him for hours, had crept into his bones.

"What is that?" Tom heard a man ask, and he

looked up the bank. The moon was near the horizon now but still bright. Two men were staring at him. He was passing them backward and quickly. He tried to sit up.

"Hey!" one of the men yelled, running after him. Tom tried to turn around, dipping the sides of the raft under and making himself colder. He tried to angle toward the bank, but the stream was much too wide and the current kept him in the middle. He took a deep breath, preparing to roll off the side and swim for the bank. Before he could, the water bubbled up beneath him and cracked his shoulders and head against a rock. He went all the way under, clutching at the foam. He was being pulled hard, and his legs swung up and under him until they banged against a rock ceiling.

For a moment, he got his face back into the air. One arm was hooked over the white raft, and the other grabbed at the rock's surface, only it wasn't just a rock. It was a rock face, almost a cliff, and he was being pulled under it. His body was already horizontal, and everything but his arms and face were under the stone. He opened his mouth to yell and swallowed frothing water. Another breath, and another mouthful of stream. The men on the bank had caught up and were now just watching. Tom's hand slipped, and he shot under, raking his arm on the lip. He spun around and bounced, grinding his cheek on the rock above him. The foam was coming with him. His fingers had dug deep into it, and they were not letting go.

Very few people can remain calm when trapped underwater. Tom kicked and thrashed as the current rolled him along the underside of the rock. Something collided hard with his ribs and knocked the last of his breath out of him. Tom realized he was going to die. With that, he calmed, floating along in the dark. Then his head found air. He gasped and clutched at the raft, trying to climb back onto it.

The water began to pour downhill.

Tom, halfway back on the foam, coughing, hacking, and sucking stale air into his lungs, was going over a waterfall blind and backward. The drop and tumble didn't last long. Another shelf ground up his legs and back, and he was under again.

Every time he went under, Tom knew it might be final. But every time, his lungs found another breath, another pocket of life. It was already dark, so he closed his eyes and hugged the foam, breathing deeply when he could. He stopped counting the collisions. Shin, shoulder, skull, knuckles, ribs all throbbed. His numb mind ignored them. He was still alive and that was all it would process: life, one breath at a time.

Eventually the ceiling lifted, and a throbbing, bruised, and retching Tom found himself drifting in a pool, his head resting on his cracked and battered raft, his arms dangling limply over the sides. The black was so complete Tom couldn't tell if his eyes were closed or open. He knew he must be very deep beneath the ridge.

He was still moving. He wouldn't have been able to tell, but a very faint light appeared ahead of him and to the left, and it was moving closer. In such heavy darkness, even a faint light can seem like a bonfire. Tom couldn't look away. It was no more than a glow, and still it showed his straining eyes the faint outline of a ceiling scattered with holes and a maze of hanging boulders dividing the water. The glow was coming from the mouth of a tunnel, and in the tunnel he saw stairs. He began swimming for the stairs too late. His arms were weak and sore. He floated past, twisting to watch the light fade behind him. He smacked into a pillar of rock and the water piled up behind him, lifting the raft and pinning him to the stone. The stream was dividing on either side of him. For a few moments, he bobbed against the rock, and then the water made its decision. He and the raft slid to one side, once again heading down a hill of water. Tom ducked his head, gripped his raft, and closed his eyes.

❖　❖　❖

In the predawn, Elizabeth woke in a panic. She was out of bed before she knew why and immediately into Tom's room. He was not in his bed and the window was open. She ran out of the house barefoot, gripping the cold rock with her toes and grabbing at her arms to keep warm. The moon was gone, but the sky was lightening in preparation for the sun. The first of the birds were already chattering in the willows and the trees on the mountain behind her. She knew somehow, just as she had known when her husband had died, that Tom was not close enough to hear her.

She still called for him.

~ three ~

THE MOUNTAIN'S
BELLY

Tom didn't know he was unconscious. He didn't know anything. He hadn't felt the rock dig through the back of his scalp and rattle his skull. He hadn't flinched when his elbows cracked on stone or bent backward when his arms caught on passing rocks.

Eventually, the foam raft found a small harbor in the wall. While the current moved on, the raft and Tom's body swirled in the slow eddy. They would turn toward the fast-falling water, and spray would rinse the blood from Tom's scalp and arms and push the raft back into the hollow in the cavern wall and through another turn.

Time and water passed until one turn swung Tom's feet out into the current. The raft hesitated, but the water was pulling, not pushing.

Tom did finally feel the cold water on his face and

the ache in his limbs. He reopened his eyes, forgetting where he was. Another collision, another small water-fall, brought back all the memory he had.

"So," Jeffrey said, "where do you want me to look?"

Elizabeth sighed. She was trying very hard not to yell. Jeffrey had come when she'd called, and he'd nodded while she'd described her early morning search along the stream and up the hill behind the house. But he had yet to look anywhere himself.

"You're a guy, you tell me," Elizabeth said. "Where would you have gone?"

"I hid in the basement once. But you don't have a basement, do you?"

"No, Jeffrey, we don't," she said. "The house is on a rock. Most people don't bother digging a basement into solid rock."

Jeffrey stared out over the small valley floor with its stream and willows. And then he looked at the ridge on the other side and up at the ridge behind the house with its small peak.

"Any more ideas?" Jeffrey asked.

"Jeffrey, why don't you just start looking? I've already looked everywhere I could think of."

"I think it's important that we do this rationally."

Elizabeth shut her eyes and took a long breath. "Jeffrey."

Jeffrey raised his hands. "No, hear me out. I have an idea. Let's walk through a number of theoretical options before we make an applied search."

"Jeffrey," Elizabeth said, standing up.

"Yes?"

"Let me know when you've figured it out. I'm going to follow the stream." Elizabeth was already walking down the stairs.

"Do you want me to call the police or local radio stations or anything?"

"Wait till I get back."

"What should I do?" Jeffrey asked.

"The laundry," Elizabeth said.

Jeffrey watched her tromp through the tall grass toward the stream, and then he got up and went inside. He couldn't find any laundry.

When Tom stopped moving, there was no light to be seen. His ride, since the eddy, had not been as wild as it had at first. He had been very rarely forced under-water, and when he had, it was only briefly. The water constantly split off into smaller streams only to boil back together and split again. And along the way, every scrape with some invisible wall, every impact with an unseen boulder, sent shocks of terror and fear through Tom's cold body.

Finally, he rode the packing foam down a last chute of water and floated out onto the great calm surface of an underground lake. In the darkness it might as well have been an ocean.

Tom relaxed his beaten body and simply floated. He assumed that at some point he would once again feel the pull of the current, once again hear the anger of the water, and would travel farther. He did not mind. He thought the only way for him to survive would be to emerge on the other side of the mountain. Or he would travel deeper and deeper into the earth until eventually he was pulled under for the last time.

The raft bumped gently against something, and this time it was not stone. It crunched, like gravel. Tom stretched out his leg and dug his toe into what could only be a beach of some kind. He might have to climb back on the foam and sail on eventually, but for now he would rest. He scrambled into water up to his ribs and struggled up the steep invisible bank, pulling the raft behind him.

If his teeth hadn't been chattering and his body shaking, he probably would have slept. But the cave was cold, and he was colder. He stretched out on the gravel and wondered if he was going to cry. He was very glad to discover that he wasn't and stretched out farther, as far as his chilled muscles would allow. The fingertips on his left hand grazed something. Something that felt like rubber.

He reached for it and found that he was holding a boot. He pulled at it, but it was stuck. Groping around, his fingers closed on an ankle.

Tom caught his breath and slid away. He heard nothing, and after a minute he felt his way back toward the body. It could be just bones, he told himself. It seemed old. The cloth of the pants had been stiff in his hands.

Tom felt like he should say something.

"Hello?" His voice cracked. "Are you awake? You're dead, aren't you?" He put his hand out to where the boot had been. Then he moved his hand up. Tom could feel that the calf was thick. Not a skeleton, he told himself. Still a body. Shouldn't it stink?

"Hello?" Tom shook it gently. He could feel that the pants had been chewed on, and for the first time he wondered what might live in caves like this. Hopefully just rats.

Tom thought about getting onto his piece of packing foam and pushing himself back out onto the lake. He didn't want to be anywhere near a corpse, but he was in a pretty bad pitch-black way, and the corpse might have something he could use. There had been stairs and a light. That meant that people came in here on purpose. Maybe this guy had come in on purpose. He might have a map of passages. Of course, Tom wouldn't be able to see a map, but then maybe this guy had brought a light.

In the end, Tom silenced his teeth and his emotions and felt for the dead man's hands and pockets. In one of the pockets he found a mushy ball of what must have been food, but nothing in or on his hands except one large ring on the man's little finger, which, after a moment's hesitation, he tried to slide off. At first, the ring wouldn't budge, then a dead knuckle popped and Tom staggered back with the ring in his hand. It was thick, with a large flat surface on one side. Tom shoved it into his pocket and then sat down to think and, in sitting, found the dead man's bag.

The bag had two shoulder straps and had obviously been wet and then dried in a funny shape. When Tom's blind fingers found the zipper, he was surprised that it opened easily. Inside, he felt a plastic bag, like the ones his mother put his sandwiches in when she packed his lunch, only bigger and heavier. It was also zipped shut. Inside that, he discovered a small pocketknife, a square can, and a stack of cold, fat metal cylinders. He didn't need his eyes to tell him what they were. Nothing feels quite like a battery.

Tom groped through the man's pockets again and then methodically felt all over the gravel beach on his hands and knees. He found only coarse sand and gravel, and neither of those uses batteries.

Tom sat beside the body, held the bag, and thought. If the man had batteries, then he had to have something that *used* batteries, and since he was going into caves, that thing would probably be a light. If he hadn't missed it when he was crawling around. Tom could only think of two possibilities. The man had either dropped his flashlight into the water or it was under his body.

Tom gathered himself, then dug his hands under the dead man's bony back and tried to roll him over. The body lifted only a few inches. Tom dropped it and was surprised by a sound. Something near the man's head had clunked. He reached up and touched the heavily bearded face, and there, above the face, was a helmet, and on the helmet was a large headlamp.

Tom felt around the lamp with his fingers and found the strap that fixed it to the helmet. But for all of his tugging, it remained solidly attached. Finally— he had come this far already—he sent his hands down into the man's beard, a flattened mat of tangled bristles, and felt for the chin strap of the helmet itself. Disgusted, he moved his shaking hands as quickly as he could, and a moment later he'd pulled the strap over the chin and through the beard. The whole helmet was loose. He once again slid away from the corpse, hoping not to learn any more about it, and began blindly searching for a way to install batteries.

Installing batteries can be impossible in full daylight. Tom was attempting it in subterranean darkness, with numb fingers. Several times he dropped the helmet and lay back against the beach to calm his frustration and rub his hands. Finally, a plastic square slid free from the top and two thick batteries dropped out. Tom kicked them toward the water and took two batteries from the stack, leaving four, which he dropped back in the bag. With clumsy fingers and an aching body, he began trying to insert the new batteries. On his third attempt, the cave came to life.

Tom blinked and shut his eyes for a moment before squinting at the brightness. The headlamp was strong, even more so to Tom's eyes in that deep cave. After a moment's hesitation, he pointed the helmet back at the body.

The man had been large, and Tom was surprised at how newly dead he looked. His skin was white and patchy blue. Tom had found dead things in his stream before and knew enough to realize that the man had not spent much time in the water after he'd died. He would have been much uglier if he had. As it was, he was hardly pretty. His neck and chest were covered by the chaotic carpet of his large beard. His hair, also long and very tangled, had hardened into the shape of the inside of the helmet. A clump of the hair was cemented to his cheekbone with blood. Tom felt in his pocket for the ring from the man's finger. It was gold, a school ring with a crest and a year. Tom slid it back in his pocket. He could give it to the police when he got out, and they might know who the man had been.

He turned the light through the cavern. Because of the dark, he had somehow assumed that the cave walls would be black, that the water would be like oil, and that the sand and gravel would be black as well. Some portions of the smooth walls were gray, but most of the surface was swirled with brown and tan and even red. The gravel he sat on was mostly quartz and to his long-blind eyes seemed to sparkle. Anyone else would have thought the place terribly dark, but it reminded Tom of high noon and lunchtime. His body was hungry. How many meals had he missed? He dug back into the man's bag and felt for the square can. It was a can of sardines. He hated sardines, but he still peeled the lid back and dropped one of the salted fish into his mouth. The taste by itself wiped out his hunger.

With a light, Tom felt less cold, less like he'd seen his last sunshine. But the light didn't fill the whole cavern, and where it missed seemed darker than ever. Trying to ignore the man who shared his beach, Tom picked up the helmet and slowly pointed it around the cave and lake again. The beach was small, but he could see more flotsam on it than just one body. There was a plastic NO TRESPASSING sign, a red fishing bob, and a small chunk of white foam.

He turned the light onto his raft. A back corner was missing. The whole thing was dented, and a crack ran across the middle. Tom looked up and around himself. He was sitting on the edge of a round pool that was fed from a dark mouth that his light wouldn't penetrate. The sound of tumbling water crept toward him from behind the darkness. At first, he couldn't see any outlet to the little lake, but then he noticed a narrow strip of black just above the water on the wall opposite him. It looked like the lake wasn't actually contained by this chamber. It stretched on, who knew how far, but the roof dropped down to just a couple feet above the surface. Tom also noticed several white rings that wrapped completely around the cave walls. He knew what they were. He'd seen lines like them, only much smaller, on rocks in the stream all the way back by his house. The rings marked different water levels. The highest watermark wasn't really a ring at all. It was a great white smudge that covered most of the ceiling.

"It fills all the way up," Tom said out loud, and was surprised at his own voice. In the spring when his own little stream bubbled brown and ran through the tall grass in the meadow, this cavern would be full to the top with angry water, tearing at the walls to make more room. He was glad it was summer.

Tom didn't want to move, but he also didn't want to waste the batteries. If he was going to leave the light on, then he should explore. And he was going to leave the light on. He was still cold, but he didn't see any way around his wet clothes apart from putting on the dead man's, and he was pretty sure that wasn't going to happen. So he stood up and stretched, running his cold hands down his battered legs and rubbing his bruised arms. Then he took the dead man's helmet and stuck it on his head, only to jerk it off in pain. He put one hand up and gently fingered the blood-caked lump on the back of his skull. His left cheekbone was badly swollen as well.

Eventually, biting his lip, he slid the helmet back on. It was too big, but the strap tightened up beneath his chin. With the spotlight staring out in front of him, he knelt by the dead man's feet, crawled out onto the foam raft, and pushed his exhausted body out onto the lake.

Elizabeth was not walking as quickly as she had when she'd started out. The sun would set in an hour or so, her legs were tired from an afternoon of tromping, and she was no longer hopeful. Tom had been playing with the foam in the stream, so she had thought he might simply be camping out beside it, somewhere down the valley just out of view. She had passed just out of view a long time ago.

She was on old Nestor's property now. He could hardly blame her for looking for her son, though he could blame her if her son had gone onto his land. Up ahead, in the sideways light, she could see men. They were standing by the stream where it piled against the cliff and spilled off into Nestor's pond. Her heart stopped on an offbeat and climbed into her throat. The men looked official. She could see Nestor's house now, and there were two state trooper cars parked in front of it.

She walked faster.

One of the men noticed her coming and turned to face her. When she was close enough, he called out.

"Can I help you, ma'am?"

She didn't want to say it. "I'm looking for my son." The way the troopers glanced at each other told her all she needed to know.

"We don't know that it was your son," one of them said, "but we got a call around lunch today. Two men said they were out here real early and saw a boy's body in the stream. They saw him get pulled under the rock."

"Who were they?" she asked.

"Don't know. They wouldn't give names. Said they'd been trespassing and didn't want Nestor after them."

She swallowed hard. "Dead?" she asked. "Was he dead when they saw him?"

The troopers glanced at each other. "They couldn't say. Dead or unconscious."

"So you're saying he's dead now?"

Neither trooper said anything. Elizabeth's hands went up to her hair, tucking loose strands behind her ears. She looked from one man to the other. They both looked away.

"Well," she finally said. "I'd like to report a missing person. Eleven-year-old boy, Thomas Hammond. Tall for his age, short brown hair, skinny. I'm his mother, Elizabeth Hammond."

Elizabeth turned and began walking back down the stream. "Thank you," she said over her shoulder.

"Ma'am?" one of the troopers said. "Mrs. Hammond. We could give you a lift. We're done here."

Elizabeth Hammond shook her head and kept walking.

~ four ~

THE SECOND SUITOR

MOUNTAIN RIVERS
CLAIM ANOTHER VICTIM

Early Saturday morning two men anonymously
reported seeing the body of a boy dragged
beneath a small cliff at the foot of Leepike
Ridge by one of the many streams in the
area. Later that day Elizabeth Hammond reported her eleven-year-old son, Thomas
Hammond, as missing.

This is only the most recent incident
involving missing persons, potential drown-
ings, and underground rivers. Ten years ago
the body of a spelunker, thought to have
entered caves near Leepike, was found
drowned in the brackish water of Lake
Blackhead, more than forty miles south.
Items belonging to other missing persons,

lost miles inland, have been found as far south as Hornbridge and have more frequently turned up in various harbors and beaches.

This latest tragedy, leaving behind a grieving mother and her fiancé, Jeffrey Veatch, once again involves the treacherous river courses peculiar to this region. Geologist Juan Bosley...

Elizabeth didn't read any more. The thoughts of Juan Bosley were, in fact, as far as she had gotten in all three of her attempts to read the newspaper article. She sat on the edge of the rock with her feet dangling. She had gone to church but hadn't listened to a word—not a word of the pastor's short little message, not a word of the singing, and not a word of what anybody said to her after. She was pretty sure there had been hugs. And Jeffrey had always been standing right there beside her, smiling sadly.

She didn't think Tom was dead. The afternoon Tom's father had died, she'd known something horrible had happened long before she'd received the phone call. She'd felt sick, like something had been erased inside her.

Jeffrey sneezed behind her. He had said that a period of denial was healthy, that it could be part of grieving. She wasn't sure why Jeffrey was even here, why he'd followed her home after church, or how he could justify telling the paper that he was her fiancé.

Jeffrey had also placed an obituary in the paper. In any normal frame of mind she would have laughed at it. According to the obituary, Tom was much loved at school, an excellent second baseman (he played third), and had cared for his mother for three years since his father's death. But better yet, he was survived by his mother, Elizabeth Hammond, and his step-fiancé, Jeffrey Veatch. She was pretty sure that step-fiancé didn't actually exist as an official relationship.

"Jeffrey," Elizabeth said without looking over her shoulder.

"Yeah?" He jumped up from where he'd been sitting on the rock, hurried over, and sat down beside her. He tried to put a hand on her shoulder, but she shrugged it off.

"You can go. I'm fine."

"I don't want you to be by yourself."

Elizabeth looked at him. "I *want* to be by myself. Please go. And you can write a letter to the paper explaining that you aren't actually Tom's step-fiancé, whatever that is." She looked back out over the valley. "You were my potential fiancé."

"But I thought—"

"I never said yes. In fact, let's just say no for now."

"Elizabeth, you know timing is not important for me. I'll be here. Always. Are you sure you want me to go?"

Elizabeth nodded. "Please."

Elizabeth heard him scuffle to his feet. He kissed the top of her head.

"I'll be back tomorrow," he said. "Or even later this afternoon. For dinner? After dinner? School doesn't start for five weeks."

She didn't look at him. She was thinking about Tom and how extremely angry she was going to be if he turned out to be hiding somewhere on the ridge. He couldn't possibly have drowned in his own creek, the creek he and the current generation of frogs and leeches had grown up in together. She should have stayed and looked at where the creek dumped against the cliff at Nestor's.

Jeffrey's little toothpaste car was gone when another trail of dust came crawling down Elizabeth's road. A white truck was kicking it up, and she watched it all the way in. When it parked, a man holding a bunch of flowers got out. He was tall, and his hair, from Elizabeth's bird's-eye perspective, looked perfectly black. He stepped out of view as he began to climb the stairs. She stood up, pushed her hair back behind her ears, and walked over to wait for him. The man, when he finally came into view, breathing heavily, was rather startling. He was tall, his shoulders were muscular, though clothed in a polo shirt (buttoned), and his jaw was sharp and dusted with two days' worth of carefully trimmed growth. Above his left eye, a long white scar ran into his hairline. Elizabeth tried not to look at it.

"Mrs. Hammond?" he asked, and his eyebrows went together and up in the middle to express stranger sympathy.

Elizabeth nodded.

"I just wanted to bring these by and give my condolences to you and your husband. It's hard, I know. Was your husband the one I saw driving away?"

"No. That was a friend. My husband died three years ago."

The man's eyebrows went further together and further up, and his scar went with them. They were a tepee now.

"I'm sorry," the man said. "I'm Phil Leiodes. We haven't met, I just saw the story in the paper—I went through something similar with my brother when I was little—and I just wanted to come by and bring you these daffodils."

Elizabeth took the flowers and smiled. They weren't daffodils. They were lilies.

"Thanks," she said.

Phil stood on one leg.

"If there's anything I can do . . . ," Phil began.

"Could you drive me out to old Nestor's?"

"Um, Nestor's? I'm not sure I've heard of it." He was rolling his eyes back like he was looking for directions in his eyebrows.

"I'll show you how to get there."

"Great," Phil said, and cut his face in half with a plastic smile.

Phil's truck had a pine tree air freshener and a diesel engine. Elizabeth got in first and watched Phil slide in behind the wheel. A tattoo of a scaled claw stuck up just above his shirt collar. Elizabeth looked away.

Phil might have been talking to her while he drove, but Elizabeth didn't respond. She just pointed out upcoming turns. When they were finally parked in front of old Nestor's house, she got out and began walking around the muddy pond. She heard Phil's door open, and she kept walking. Then she heard Nestor's screen door slam and dogs start barking.

"Who's that?" Nestor's voice got lost in all the noise.

"Mr. Nestor," Phil said. "It's Elizabeth Hammond."

"You don't look like no Elizabeth," Nestor said. "You're one of those treasure grubbers that's always snitchin' around on my ridge. Leiodes or some such? I called you in for trespassin' last month. What's Elizabeth doin' with a tick like you?"

"I'm just giving her a ride out here."

Elizabeth tried to ignore the conversation and the barking and made her way to where the stream crashed into the base of the ridge. Some of it went under, and some spilled back toward her and into the pond.

A golden retriever passed her on the right. She could tell other dogs were on her heels, and then three of them were all around and in front of her, jumping and barking and chewing on her pant legs. She ignored them and stopped on the bank.

It looked strangely small, just a small stream with a small current going under a big rock. She almost wanted to swim out just to see how hard it pulled.

"Don't know anything good two fellas would be up to out here before sunup," Nestor announced in her ear. He was wearing overalls and eating an apple. His white beard was stained nicotine yellow. "Can't trust trespassers to tell the truth neither," he said loudly.

Elizabeth glanced back over her shoulder. Phil was standing behind Nestor, just out of his vision, making faces at the dogs.

"Hello, Mr. Nestor," Elizabeth said. "I don't think my boy went under here. He is a good swimmer."

"Thought they said he was drowned already," Nestor said, chewing on his apple. "That's what the paper said, but the paper's all lies anyhow."

"Yes," she said. "Of course, I don't know where he is. But I don't think he drowned."

"Why not?" Phil asked. "If he went in there, he's pretty much sure to be."

"I don't know," Nestor said. "I don't mean to raise false hopes—your boy's more than likely dead and bobbin'—but I have seen animals come outta there alive." The old man paused, chewing. Elizabeth watched him. "Two years back, Goldie got sucked on down there. I thought she was gone for good, but three weeks later she was pushin' out her litter on my kitchen floor. Course, she won't go anywhere near water since. But Argus has been in a coupla times and doesn't seem worse for it."

"Is Argus a dog?" Elizabeth asked.

Nestor pulled at his nose. "Not sure what else I'd call him. Gus ain't mine. He's just sort of around. Had a collar when he got here but lost it here or there. Sleeps on the porch with the others sometimes, out here other times, and sometimes just disappears for a month or so. Last time I saw him sucked through was right after breakfast."

"This morning?" Phil asked.

"Last summer. He's limped since, but he's sure to

be around. Worthless dog." Mr. Nestor took the last bite of his apple, then began yelling. "Gus! Get on down here, dog."

"Do you need to see more?" Phil whispered. Elizabeth was surprised to find him at her ear. Everyone seemed to want to talk straight into her head.

"No," she said. "Not really. We can go in a minute."

"Hey there, Gus," Nestor said. A short, wide-bodied dog was run-limping toward them. "The rest of you, git." Nestor ran around kicking at the other dogs. They scattered, only to loop back just out of his leg's reach. "Here ya go, Gus." Nestor turned toward the stream and, much to Elizabeth's surprise, threw his apple core at the bubbling water beneath the cliff.

Even more surprising was Gus. All the dogs ran to the bank. Only Gus plunged in, paddling hard in search of the core. The core was long gone, but Gus kept paddling. Elizabeth's mouth hung open. The current caught the dog and spun him around. He was swimming against the stream now. The stream was stronger, pushing him back against the rock. His tail was in the air for a moment. Then there was nothing but a pair of ears, and Gus was gone.

"Dumb dog," Nestor muttered. "Anyhow, Mrs. Hammond, I do wish you luck findin' your boy and condolences otherwise." Nestor looked at Phil. "And you, fella, I'm hopin' not to see you anytime."

The truck ride back was mostly silent, beyond the diesel roar and spitting gravel. Elizabeth tried not to look at Phil, keeping her eyes on the road or out her window. Nestor was a strange old man, but her husband had always liked him for some odd reason, like he was looking forward to getting old, just so he could spit and yell at trespassers and wear ratty overalls like Nestor.

That hadn't happened.

"Guy's senile," Phil said, and it took a moment for Elizabeth to realize that he'd spoken.

"What?" she finally asked.

"I said he's senile. I didn't know his name, but last month he caught me hiking on part of the ridge that's apparently his, and he tried to shoot me with his shotgun. Then he called the cops."

"It's just rock salt," Elizabeth said. "He loads shells with rock salt. It won't kill you. It just buries into your skin and burns really bad."

"Well that's good then," Phil said. "No worries now. I'll just wear goggles when I hike."

Elizabeth laughed. "And it scars nasty," she said. "At least that's what I've heard."

Elizabeth watched her tall rock with its house hat coming closer. When the truck stopped, she opened her door and dropped out to the gravel.

"Mr. Leiodes," she said.

"Phil."

"Phil. Thank you for driving me. Tom is alive." Elizabeth shut the door and walked up the stairs.

It hadn't taken long for everyone to assemble. Phil made one call after dropping Elizabeth off, then drove into town and parked at the back entrance of the bowling alley.

The door was all battered metal and had no handle. Phil kicked it twice and stood back. When it opened, a man with a long pale face, lank black hair, and round-lensed glasses stared at him. Without a word, the man turned and disappeared into the dark room.

Phil stepped over the threshold, the metal door clanging shut behind him. He followed the man through the dark by the sound of his shuffling feet. Then another door opened, and the man's descending shape was framed against a lit stairwell. Phil felt his way onto the sighing, crooked steps and into the cool, dank-smelling room below. It was his first time in the bowling alley basement in almost two years.

The only light in the basement room came from the stairwell and from six glowing cigarettes. Phil could see the ring of twelve chairs around the edge of the room, and he knew only six would ever be filled. The other six were left empty for missing and dead members.

Phil didn't sit down. He would wait for an invitation.

The man who'd let him in sat down next to his identical brother. Both men were long-faced and lankhaired, and both had cigarette glow reflecting off their glasses. Beside them sat a wide cop with a hand on his gun belt. On the far side of the ring of chairs sat a huge man, his legs sprawling in the light from the stairs. His face was in shadow.

"Sit," the man said.

Phil sat down across from the twins, beside a tall man with an eye patch hunching in his chair.

The huge sprawling man rattled open a tin of breath mints, dumping a few into his hand. He tossed them into his mouth, took a long draw on his cigarette, and flicked the ash onto the floor.

"Well?" he said.

Phil cleared his throat. His leg was bouncing.

"She's not a grieving mother at all. She's sure he's alive." Suddenly the room throbbed with thunder. Phil jumped. The thunder rolled slowly across the ceiling, followed by a crash and tumbling ten times as loud when the bowling pins scattered. Phil blushed, hoping that no one could see.

The cop shifted in his seat. "Big Lotus says you think the boy went in on purpose," he said. He was thick, and his belt and uniform made him look thicker. They called him Sirens. "Is that all you got? That she's not grieving?" He turned to the twins. "What you fellas think?"

The two of them glanced at each other. One of them spoke. "We lowered Pook and Cy into the cave and were standing down by the creek to keep a spot on Nestor when this kid floats by. He sat up right before the rock face and caught himself with one arm, got a good hold of his little white raft, and then pulled it under with him. Could have been an accident. Could have been on purpose. He didn't yell for help or nothin', and he seemed pretty collected."

Thunder rolled across the ceiling again. The men all sat quietly until the pins scattered.

"Pook?" the big man asked.

A little man leaned forward out of the big man's shadow.

"I told Lotus this already," Pook said. "Me and Cy were on the stairs most of the night, and we didn't see anything. The kid could be dead, or he might know something we don't. He might be somewhere we haven't been."

Lotus, legs still sprawling, pointed his cigarette at Phil. "You mind givin' us a minute." He wasn't asking.

Phil climbed back up the stairs, sat on the floor in

the dark, and listened to the bowling thunder roll. Finally the door at the top of the stairs opened and Cy, the tall man with the eye patch, nodded at him.

In the basement, Phil was not invited to sit again. He stood and watched more mints and smoke travel down Lotus's throat.

"Phil," the big man finally said. "We need to know what she knows. And if that boy's after treasure, we need to find him or it first. We're not offering you your seat back yet, or your share, but if you get us something we can use, that sorta thing could happen." Lotus straightened, giving Phil his first good look at the man's thick lips and purple blotchy face.

Lotus grinned. "Do what ya gotta do."

~ five ~

DARK ENCOUNTER

Throughout time, many people have decided they would rather die than keep running or climbing or walking. Tom was approaching just such a decision. He was so bone weary that he found his eyelids literally clamping shut and his limbs refusing to move. Adrenaline had cost him a great deal, and with a body empty of all energy, he had set out to explore the cavern one more time. Just one more lap around the walls, and he would allow himself to sleep on the little beach with the dead man.

Part of the reason for paddling around on the lake had been to look for outlets. Part had been a desire to be away from the dead man. Part had been a simple justification for using up batteries. If he was going to be resting, then he knew he should turn the headlamp off. He was now prepared to do that. He was prepared to sleep on the dead body if necessary. So he lifted his arms one at a time, and he clawed his way through the water, trying to cross the lake to where he knew the beach was and where he knew he could finally sleep.

Tom was putting his head down, resting his neck just for a moment, when the raft bumped, rocking in a slow circle. He whipped his head around, raking the surface of the water with the light, and suddenly his arms were flailing. He splashed, tipped, tried to right himself, but the foam flipped and he was in the water. His head, helmet, and lamp went under and then reemerged. The light remained strong.

He kicked out, swimming toward the bank, dragging the raft with him. It was probably only a log, he told himself. Calm down and breathe. Just a log. Then his legs cramped, and he was under again. Gripping the raft, he tried to pull himself above the surface, but he felt the foam cracking. It was going to break in half.

His light flickered and went out.

The packing foam moved in his arm, pushing against him. Something was clawing at it from the other side.

Tom's legs forgot their cramps, and he kicked and surged up out of the water and onto his now invisible raft. He swam hard, leaving his hands in the water as little as possible. And when that last emergency store of adrenaline was gone and his lungs were burning, his raft crunched into sand and gravel.

Tom felt no safer once he was on firm ground. The bumping thing in the water might be able to come out of it. He scrambled all the way up the bank, pressed his back against the cavern wall, pulled his helmet off, and fumbled with the plastic, trying to get the batteries out, hoping the insides of the lamp just needed to dry.

Tom never doubted that he could stay awake forever and fight and bite and kick whatever came out of the water at him. And that is when he fell asleep, with knees pulled to his chest, two batteries in his right hand, a blind helmet in his left, a dead man not ten feet away, and something in the water.

Tom was sitting in the corner of the kitchen with his knees against his chest. For some reason he was cold. His father walked around him.

"Beth!" he yelled. "Baby, where'd you put the griddle?"

"I didn't put it anywhere!" Elizabeth's voice called back. "Have you looked in its home? Where it lives? Where it's been every other time you've looked for it?"

Ted Hammond looked around himself. Tom stared up at his dad's arms and into his eyes.

"Where's that?" Ted finally yelled again.

"In the cupboard by the stove."

"I already looked there."

"Look again."

Tom's back was against the door to the cupboard beside the stove. Ted bent over and smiled at him. He put his hand on his son's head and slapped his cheek gently. Tom started to move out of the way but then saw that his father had somehow reached past him and was already plugging the griddle in on the counter.

"Was it there?" his mother yelled.

"Nope. It was in the cupboard by the stove." Ted was smiling. Elizabeth didn't say anything for a moment.

"Are you trying to be funny?" she finally asked.

"No," Ted said with a laugh. "I *am* being funny."

Tom was still cold, but he was smiling now. His mom walked around the corner, and his dad picked her up the way he always did when he kissed her.

"Should we wake Tom?" she asked.

"No. He's growing. Let him sleep. The smell will wake him soon enough."

And then the two of them cooked.

Ted Hammond fried bacon and then ham. He fried up cowboy potatoes and mixed them with eggs and cheese and onions and fried up the whole mess. He made Elizabeth a veggie omelet. When he finished with the savory, he began working on the sweet. Thick buttermilk pancakes, French toast, and cinnamon rolls.

The hunger was what woke Tom. Or maybe it was the scuffling on the beach. Either way, he opened his eyes, then tried to open them again because he thought they were still shut. A piercing pain was twisting through his gut, and his mouth was a pool of saliva. Was he in the closet? Why was it so dark? He hoped his dad hadn't eaten all the food. His ears were hearing something, something that didn't fit. And the darkness didn't fit either. Scuffling sounds in the dark, and why was he cold? His clothes were all wet.

When memory came, it came suddenly and completely. There had been something in the water. Now there was something scuffling on the beach beside him.

Tom held his breath. Was the dead man alive? What would he do to a boy who had picked through his pockets and taken his helmet? But Tom had felt his cold neck. He had popped his knuckle and pulled his ring. He was dead. Had something come out of the water? Was it eating the dead man?

Tom shivered. The batteries were still in his hand. As silently as he could, he fitted the batteries into the little box. As the lid clicked into place, the beach lit up. Tom blinked.

The dead man's body had moved. Tom ran the light over a long, smooth track in the gravel. Two wide eyes flashed the light back. Some sort of crawling animal had the dead man's arm in its mouth. It was dragging the body along the beach. Tom grabbed a handful of gravel and threw it. His arm was stiff, and the rocks fell short.

The animal stood up and stared at him. It was short, but its body was wide. A tail wagged. The creature hopped over the man and limped toward Tom.

"Are you a dog?" Tom asked.

Argus shoved his nose into Tom's face. If Tom hadn't already known the answer, the dog's licking would have told him. Even though he was still hopelessly lost, Tom smiled and almost felt warmer. A dog was much better company than a dead man.

Tom rubbed the dog's ears and pulled his hands away sticky. He turned the light to the dog's fur and saw that its scalp was matted with blood. A big gash ran down the center of its head. The dog didn't seem to mind. He was all tongue and wagging tail.

"I can't do anything about that," Tom said, and wiped the blood on his pants. "What were you doing with him? You weren't trying to eat him, were you? Were you trying to wake him up? He's dead. He won't wake up. But he had some fish."

Tom's stomach was forcing its way back into the

spotlight. Tom unzipped the bag and found the sardines. He ate one, and this time he enjoyed it. He gave one to the dog. Argus gulped it back like a seal and sat staring at Tom, hoping there would be more. The sardines went back in the bag.

Gus was sad to see them go.

In the dark, time crawls like a tired snail. When a belly is growling, it slows to a near stop. For Tom, time no longer existed. There were no stars, no sun, no breeze, no chirruping crickets or calling mother. He couldn't even track the periods of the day by his hunger because his hunger was constant. For a while, with the thick, limping dog as a friend, the weight of time lifted. There was something to look at that was moving. There was a sound to listen to besides the constant pouring of water that echoed through the cave. But while Tom sat with his back against the cave wall and his hand gripping the loose skin on the dog's back, he didn't think of the life of his batteries. The helmet rested on the gravel beside the two of them, pointing away from the corpse, leaving it in shadow.

Tom didn't really need the light; he was just thinking. But he left it on. He stared around the cavern walls, listening to Gus chew on a waterlogged stick.

If he had a bottle and something to write on, he could send a message. What would he say? "Hey, Mom,

I'm stuck inside a mountain on an underground lake with a dog. Come get me."

He wouldn't last long on a couple of sardines. At least I've got plenty to drink, he thought.

As if reading his mind, Gus stood and limped down to the water. He lapped up his black drink and wandered off into the dark.

"Where you going?" Tom asked, and turned the helmet toward the dog. "Don't do that."

Argus was pulling the body around again. Tom put the helmet on his head and walked over.

"Drop it!" He tried to pull the man's foot out of the dog's mouth. Argus raised his hackles and growled, but his tail was wagging. He was happy to play tug-of-war with the man's body. Tom tugged harder, and Gus dropped the boot and jumped around playfully on his three good legs. Tom wasn't paying attention. He was staring at the boot. The dog's teeth had left deep scratches on the leather toe.

Tom felt around in the gravel until he found a small sharp rock, and then he began unlacing the man's boot. Argus sat back to scratch himself and chew on his gimpy leg. When the boot came off, Tom sat back hard and scooted away quickly. There was a terrible smell. It was the smell of decay.

Trying to ignore it, Tom moved farther away and

propped the boot between his knees. Taking his sharp rock, he began to work. Several minutes later he had managed to scrawl around the toe I'M ALIVE STUCK. He had been planning on adding UNDERGROUND LAKE, but it wasn't even going to come close to fitting. Instead he added his initials, TH. He stared at the boot for a while and decided there wasn't much more he could say about his situation. He stood up and walked to the black water. He swung his arm around a couple times to loosen his shoulder, stepped forward, and hurled the boot as far into the water as he could.

Argus hit the water before the boot landed.

"Hey! No!" Tom yelled, but it didn't matter. The boot immediately sank.

Tom sat back down and rubbed his fingertips, sore from pinching the small rock. Argus approached the spot where the boot had gone to its watery grave and snorted around, surveying the situation. Tom once again looked over the walls, staring at the high-water marks and the pocks and dents in the rock. Some of them might lead to other chambers, but they were all too high to reach from the water. There was also the lower-ceilinged part of the cavern. He could try his luck there. Of course, once he tried, the current wouldn't let him come back. He didn't have a rope to tie off to anything, so he would just have to hope that he would be as lucky as he had been so far. There were no guarantees of air. If he was pushed under, it could be forever.

He took out another sardine and bit its head off. If he got hungry enough, he would risk the current and the low ceiling. He didn't want to die next to a decaying body. He held on to the sardine tail, waiting for the thick dog paddling back to him. He even whistled, and as he whistled, his light dimmed and became orange.

In a panic, Tom grabbed at the helmet, twisted the lamp, and darkness reclaimed the cavern. Tom flopped onto his back, irritated with himself and once more afraid. The dog brought some comfort and some sanity, but he was only a friend to die with, or to chew on his arm after he'd died. Tom listened to the wet dog climb up the bank. Its cold nose found the fish tail in Tom's hand. Even with the scent of dog right next to it, Tom's nose picked up the other smell it had found and refused to forget, the smell of decay.

Argus didn't stay beside him long. The dog stood, and moments later Tom heard the sound of a body being tugged around on gravel. Tom grabbed another fistful of rocks and threw them into the darkness.

"Stop it!"

Argus did stop for a moment. He cocked his head and sniffed, curious why the boy was throwing gravel.

Then the man's sleeve went back in his mouth, and he continued sweeping the small beach with the body. He was not a selfish dog, though, and this dead thing was interesting enough for both of them. He shifted position and began dragging the man toward Tom.

Tom was trying hard to ignore the noise, but he couldn't pretend it wasn't getting closer when Gus's rear legs stepped on him and then over him.

"No." Tom sat up and broke the dog's grip. He twisted on the dim orange light, grabbed the man's arms, and pulled him down the beach. Argus jumped around the man's feet, barking happily. When the man's head and hands were in the water, Tom moved around to his feet, pushed him out, and stepped back. The man floated. He sank in spots, but in general he was floating. Tom lunged after him and pulled his leg back onto the beach. Gus tried to help and got a push for his effort. Tom felt around for another sharp rock and then burst out laughing.

"I'm an idiot," he said out loud. He dropped the leg, retrieved the man's bag, and dug out the knife. It was a small, silver-handled, three-bladed pocketknife and much better than a rock. Tom etched TOM'S ALIVE onto the toe of the other boot, even including the apostrophe, and pushed the body out once more. Feeling suddenly more affectionate toward the man, Tom thought he should say something.

"Dust to dust" was all that came, a memory from another funeral, a memorial service with green and pink mints to commemorate the passing of his father and no body to actually put in the dirt. Then, comfortable for the first time on his little plot of beach, Tom lay down, tucked the bag beneath his head, turned off the dying light, and whistled for Argus. The dog didn't come at once but stood staring into the darkness with his nose, considering whether or not the man could be retrieved. When he did come, Tom threw his arm around the wet dog.

"I'm glad he's gone," Tom said. His aching body relaxed, and his mind, relieved at the dead man's departure, tumbled into sleep.

Argus didn't sleep at first, even though there were no distractions now, at least none he could chew on. He dropped his chin onto the beach and flared his nostrils at the slowly passing water and Tom's sardine-flavored snoring. When he did sleep, his dreams involved apple cores, boots that didn't sink, and bodies that stayed on beaches.

Tom stirred.

"Maybe waffles," he muttered.

~ SIX ~

SKY WATER

From the top of the chimney where Elizabeth sat, the weaving van had been visible for several minutes. After an initial glance, she hadn't looked back. She was outside, staring at the sky and smelling the breeze. She didn't know exactly which of the ladies from town would be in the van, but she knew what they would have to say, and she had already had her fill of visitors for the day.

While Tom and Argus were launching a dead man on his final voyage, Elizabeth had greeted her first visitors of the morning and accepted their condolences. They were mothers of Tom's classmates, girls from work and their sisters. They had come in one big group to overwhelm her grief with numbers. They had offered to do laundry, but there had been no laundry, to do the dishes, but she hadn't eaten. In the end, some of them had swept and vacuumed already clean floors while others sat with her and smiled sadly.

Hope was not something her visitors were equipped to handle, so she didn't tell them she thought Tom was alive. She merely thanked them, smiled, and even accepted some of the hugs.

At first, she had answered the phone because it might be the sheriff, but now she never did. "It might be the sheriff" had always been Jeffrey breathing and making kissy noises or women speaking in quiet voices, offering more artificial assistance—food, condolences. Casseroles and sympathy couldn't find her son.

While this newest van stopped at the base of the stairs, Tom slept with his arm around a wet dog and Elizabeth stared at the sky and the big-bellied clouds. The phone was ringing again, somewhere below her, and she knew it was going to rain. The smell in the air could have told her that, even if she couldn't see the sky. The clouds above her were barely gray and scattered, but the horizon was lined with giants, real black-hearted, flat-bottomed storm clouds.

When Tom climbed onto the roof, he always scurried up in two moments and then set himself on the chimney. For his mother, getting from the chain to the roof to the peak had taken much longer. Now that she was up there, sitting on one edge of the chimney, she didn't want to move. This was Tom's perspective on the world, had probably been his father's as well. Sitting there, she felt closer to both of them, closer and still achingly distant.

The willows were sweeping the ground and stirring the stream's surface, collecting themselves in the breeze and preparing for a real summertime blow. The meadow grass rippled and rolled around the valley floor like a green-bladed spring flood. Elizabeth could hear the last storm-brave cicadas in the trees and the constant percussion of the leaves. The view was only twenty feet higher than the view that she loved out her kitchen window, but here there was no glass. There were no walls and no real floor. It was a bird's perch, and the view went all the way around and all the way up, from ridge to ridge and back again, from stream to stars, hiding behind clouds and daylight. She would come back up here on a clear night if she didn't think she would fall on the way.

In all of it, in all the smells and feels that tumbled through Elizabeth's head, there came the sound of heavy breathing, footsteps on the stairs, and old women from the van complaining. Tom's mother did what Tom would have done. She ignored them. They banged on the door. They talked and they yelled for her, but she didn't listen. They went inside and she didn't care. The clouds were still there for her to watch, and there was plenty for her to think about.

She saw Phil's truck at the same time the tumbling thunder first rolled through the valley. The big truck was fishtailing around the bends and throwing up a lot of gravel. The women came out of the house and waited, and Elizabeth waited above them. Phil's truck soon slid to a stop, and he ran up the whole flight of steps. He was carrying a casserole.

"You Phil?" one of the women asked. Elizabeth saw him run his free hand through his black hair and nod his surprise. She wondered if he would look up. "What are you doing around Elizabeth Hammond's place?"

"I made her some dinner," Phil said. "She's lost her son."

"She's not home," the woman said.

The sky crackled with a flash as fat rain bounced off the rock. Elizabeth looked straight up. She could hear the women hurrying down the stairs.

She heard the door open below her. Phil had gone inside. He was calling her name.

The rain was coming hard, stinging her bare arms. The rain and wind were better than a ringing phone and visitors with casseroles.

The lightning changed her mind.

She watched the clouds flicker as the bursts and flashes hopped around the sky. Then forks began falling to the ground. Three thick branches of light dove to the ridge across the valley and converged on a fir tree. The thunder shook the house almost simultaneously. Another flash blinked behind Elizabeth, and the burst of sound nearly knocked her off the chimney. For a split second she thought about standing up and stretching her hands toward the sky, but only for a split second. It came from sitting on the chimney, from being Tom's mother.

She stood beneath the heavy clouds as they solidified and fell to the ground. Phil or no Phil, she was going inside to unplug the appliances. If Tom came back, she didn't want to be ovenless with a fridge full of bad milk. The old wooden shakes on the roof were at their slickest, so she sat down to scoot carefully.

There would be no scooting.

Elizabeth slid down the slope of the roof, filling the heels of her hands with wet splinters as she went. She caught the chain as she dropped off the edge and dangled with a throbbing strained forearm. Before she could think to drop, the kitchen door burst open and Phil ran out into the rain. If he had turned, he would have seen her dangling there. His casserole was tucked under one arm and his head was down in the rain. Under his other arm he carried a narrow wooden box. On the end of the box were the initials TDH. They stood for Theodore Dolius Hammond. The box contained souvenirs of her dead husband's life. It had been hidden behind the sweaters on the top shelf of her closet.

Elizabeth forgot the rain and the lightning and the wind. She forgot she was dangling and dropped heavily to the rock below. She picked herself up and walked to the edge of the stairs and stood still, watching Phil's truck swing around and then disappear. When the truck was gone, she sat and, for the first time in a very long while, began to cry. She sat there until she saw another car winding down her road. Then she stood up and went inside. She locked the door, didn't answer the ringing phone, and, despite all of the lightning-storm wisdom of her mother, she got into the shower. She made it as hot as she could stand.

When she got out with red skin, she stared at the top shelf of her closet. The sleeve of an old blue sweatshirt that had belonged to Tom's father was dangling out of a pile of disturbed clothing. She pulled it down. NAVY CREW it said in white cracked letters.

She put it on even though her hands didn't reach out of the arms, and she went and stood at her kitchen window, staring down at the windblown willow heads shaking like dogs trying to shed the fast-falling water.

"Thomas Hammond," she said out loud. "You come home right now."

❀   ❀   ❀

Argus was gone.

Tom woke up flat on his face in the gravel. His legs were in the lake and the water was pulling at them. He twisted and sat up. The cavern was roaring. He felt around for the helmet and turned it on. The faint orange light showed him a different cave. His gravel beach was less than half its former size. The water level had gone up at least two feet, and the lake didn't look like a lake. The surface of the water was moving like a river, and the beach was slowly sliding into it.

The other side of the lake no longer had a low ceiling. Where the lip of the overhang had been, water boiled up against the cavern wall. The dark mouth that had hidden its chute of water was now overwhelmed. Muddy white water surged through it, filling the cavern with its glut. Tom looked around for the dog. Argus was standing at the other end of the much-shorter beach. His tail was down between his legs. Tom was glad to see him.

The foam raft, however, was nowhere to be seen.

Tom was trying to keep his breathing even. He stood up, strapped the helmet on, and put the bag over his shoulder. He didn't know what could bring all this new water. Of course, he didn't need to know what did it. He needed to decide what to do and he needed to decide now.

Tom drew a line in the gravel about a foot up the

beach from the water. He turned his light off and counted to one hundred. When he turned the light back on, there were only two inches of gravel left. He drew another line and counted to five hundred. The water erased the first line and was halfway to the second.

Tom looked at the froth-topped lake, and his heart beat faster. His throat was constricting. He was not yet struggling, not yet fighting this current, but he knew that he soon would be, and he knew what that meant. He hadn't been able to pull himself out of the creek when it had first sucked him under, and that current was nothing to this. He had no raft now, his bones were bruised and aching, and his skull still throbbed under the tangled scab on the back of his head.

He whistled to Argus. The dog didn't come until Tom got out the sardines. Together they ate the last two salty fish. Tom threw the empty tin into the water. Gus didn't chase it. The dying batteries followed soon after, then two of the four remaining batteries brightened up the swirling surface.

He scanned the lake, hoping to spot his raft, but there was too much chopping water for him to see anything. With only two feet of beach left, Tom placed his toes ten inches from the moving waterline with his back toward the wall and turned off his light. In the darkness, he could feel the sandy ground moving beneath him.

When the water was licking his toes, he turned the lamp back on and stepped in.

"See ya, dog," he said, and Argus watched him wade into the moving lake. The drop had been steep before, and the fast-moving water made it steeper now. When he was in up to his thighs, Tom could hardly stand. One more step and the water pulled his feet out from under him and he was off, treading water, trying to keep his head above the surface, watching for the foam raft. The dog only hesitated a moment before bobbing along behind.

Tom knew where he would end up, and he hoped that his raft would be floating there, waiting for him. He didn't think his chances were good. It was probably already drifting in the ocean.

His light flashed around the cave almost too quickly for him to focus on anything. Foam and black water rolled around him, sweeping him toward the cave wall. As he reached it, Tom felt the water below pulling him down while the surface pushed him up, piling and splashing against the stone. He kicked and pushed up as hard as he could before the current slammed him against the rock. The surface was smooth but porous and pockmarked, chewed on and then sanded by the water. Tom found a grip with both hands and held on, trying to regain his breath while his knees banged against the lip of the overhang beneath him.

Blinking spray out of his eyes while both spitting and drinking water, Tom leaned back from the rock as far as he could and looked down the length of the wall. Not more than fifteen feet away, beaten flat against the rock, he saw his white brick.

Tom gripped the wall harder than he had ever gripped anything, ignoring the strain in his forearms and fingers, and pulled himself toward the surging packing foam. When he was within reach, he tested himself, holding on to the wall with one hand, and then he began to lean.

Argus collided with him from behind. The dog slid down under Tom and into the crooks of his knees. Tom locked his legs against the current, hung on with one hand, and felt for the dog with the other. He gripped Gus's loose flesh hard enough to break the dog's skin with his fingernails and then heaved with his whole body. Argus's front legs and head landed on the raft. With a boost, the dog went all the way up.

Tom managed to get his upper body on behind the dog, dragging his legs and keeping a firm, one-handed grip on the wall.

Tom looked around the cave, spat out as much water as he could, and blinked his eyes clear. He was alive. He almost hadn't been, but he was. He wondered if he should turn the light off for a little. He decided against it and then noticed the bigger pockmarks in the cavern walls. Before the flood, they'd been too high to reach from the water's surface. Now the water level had risen. Tom scanned the rock, trying to estimate height. They still looked too high to reach. One small, dark gash caught his attention, a crack in the wall that ran down from the ceiling. It didn't reach the water, though it was much closer than the others.

There were no other possibilities, so Tom began pulling his way around the cave, hand over hand. By the time he approached the dark mouth, the top half of him was actually hot, and Argus was curled up licking sweat off his face.

The crack was big enough for Tom, but not for the raft. The water pouring out of it was only a few inches deep. Tom pushed Gus in, and the dog stood easily. Tom followed. He watched the packing foam float back onto the lake. Then he turned and began crawling in the shallow water.

The water grew even shallower as the stone floor climbed up steeply. Then the floor leveled and twisted and began to descend. Trickles came through the walls, and the water on the floor deepened, moving quickly.

Tom crawled for as long as he could, sometimes taking his bag off and squeezing through narrower cracks and sometimes lifting Argus up through the wider spots when the bottom was too narrow. When his knees could no longer take it, he turned off his light and lay down, with the water running around his body, until he could talk himself into continuing. At one point the ceiling got so low he had to push his bag and helmet through first. On the other side, he grabbed the crying and whining Argus by the front legs and pulled him yelping through.

The tunnel widened, but it also filled. The farther he went, the steeper it became and the more water poured in from the walls and ceiling. Finally Tom stopped and stared down the steepest drop yet. It looked like a waterslide lined with rocks and with no lifeguard at the bottom. Tom told himself that it leveled out a few feet below and began inching his way down feetfirst. Behind him, Argus slipped and hit him between the shoulder blades. It was all he needed.

Tom's hands slid and his heels skidded. He was dropping, leaning back on the dog's body. He threw his arms up to protect his face and cracked his elbow on the ceiling. The tunnel didn't level out a few feet below. It spat them into a small waterfall and tumbled them over backward.

Tom was underwater. His arm was caught in something. He tried to pull his head up, but the helmet was caught too. He kicked and thrashed and only managed to entangle his other arm. As his feet splashed on the surface, Tom heard something metal banging. His limbs were burning. His muscles had no oxygen. And then he relaxed. He swallowed once, and then again, and his stomach could hold no more water. He needed to breathe, but his lungs couldn't find anything. They tried anyway. He gasped. The water poured in and his chest felt like it was ripping open. His mind didn't care. There's that metal sound again, he thought.

Tom didn't feel the large hand grip his bag and sweatshirt together, and he didn't notice when he was pulled out onto a flat rock and dropped.

His body was there, but Thomas Hammond was no longer inside it.

~ seven ~

KING FISHER

Tom's body threw up a lot of water. With heavy hands pumping and pressing it, his body hacked, coughed, and spewed. Air was forced into waterlogged lungs as water spilled out and ran down the rock.

"Hey, Dad," Tom said. He didn't have his helmet on, and he was dry. "Where's Mom?"

"She's still at home," his father said. He was standing in a small doorway. His hand was on the latch.

"Is she coming?"

"Not yet."

"Can I come in and wait for her?"

"Not yet." Ted Hammond smiled, and then, slowly, he stepped back and shut the door.

❖ ❖ ❖

Someone was crushing Tom's chest, and he was vomiting. There was a yelping too, almost a barking. Someone was holding him up now. Tom wondered if he was on fire. His insides were burning, but water was dripping off of him onto the rock. Maybe someone had put him out. Then he was dropped. He smacked heavily onto the stone floor. The yelping stopped. There was light in this place, but it was orange and unsteady. There were also two large bare feet.

"Argus, you old dog. Did you think I needed a boy?"

The voice echoed in Tom's head. Then there was laughter, lots of laughter, and the sounds a man makes when he is talking to a dog. Tom rolled himself onto his side and looked up.

The man dropped to the floor beside an excited Argus, lit by firelight. His bare legs were long and lean. He was wearing some sort of cutoff shorts and no shirt. His ribs stood out, and he seemed all bone and muscle. His shoulders, neck, and arms were taut, and his back rippled while he rubbed the wet dog. The man turned where he was sitting and looked at Tom—and even while he was panting and just barely on the right side of life, Tom was surprised by the brightness of the man's eyes and by the black beard that ran down his chest in a thick braid. The hair on the man's head was not long at all, cut unevenly and sticking out from his head in all directions. Argus was lying on his back getting his belly rubbed.

"You're still alive, if you're wondering," the man said, and smiled. "I'm Reg. Apparently you already know Argus."

"Argus?" Tom asked.

"My dog. His name is Argus. I haven't seen him in quite a while. Thanks for bringing him by."

"Sure," Tom said, not knowing what else to say. Then he sat all the way up, coughing and dizzy. As his head began to clear, he looked around the cave. The walls were covered with carvings. There were smooth stone columns cut out from the rock, a few of them unbroken but most split or cracked, and there were several stone bowls. In each of them a fire flickered.

"How long have you been down here?" Tom asked.

Reg glanced at the columns and laughed. "Oh, I didn't do all this. I've done a few things, the man who lived here before me did a few things, but most of it was done a very long time ago."

"But how long have you been down here?"

Reg ran his hand down his beard braid. "A little more than three years. Not all of it was spent in here." He waved his hand around the chamber. "But most of it was."

"Three years?" Tom asked, and staggered to his feet, wobbling. "Isn't there any way out?"

"Oh, I'm sure there's a way out, I just haven't been able to find one. But that's why I keep eating." Reg thumped Argus on the belly and then stood up carefully, favoring his right leg. He was tall, but not as tall as he had looked at first. "You haven't told me your name yet. As you'll probably be living here with me for a while, it would be good to start on the right foot. Like I already said, I'm Reg." He stuck out his hand, and Tom shook it.

"I'm Tom," he said. "Thanks for saving me."

"Thanks for bringing my dog. I'm glad the flood hadn't washed my net down yet, or you would have dropped quite a ways. That little pool you were in spills a couple hundred feet down."

"Your net? What do you mean?"

Reg limped across the room toward a rough arched doorway and the sound of the water. Argus limped behind him. Tom followed carefully, trying not to slip on the smooth, wet stone. Every breath burned his lungs and brought more hacking. He threw up while Reg picked up a thick stick from a stack leaning against the wall.

"The chucks will probably keep coming for a little while," he said. "Just don't make any sudden movements." One end of Reg's stick was wrapped in something white. He dipped it into one of the fire-bowls, then held it up through the arched doorway. The light the torch gave off wasn't bright, but it was enough to illuminate the small, turbulent chamber. Across from them was a solid stone wall. On the right, water was dumping into a pool from three separate inlets. The pool was boiling with the violence of the falling water. Tom couldn't believe that he'd been in it. Or that he'd come out. Water spilled out at the left side of the pool, passing through a fencelike tangled and ripped mess. On either end a cluster of small cans banged and rattled together.

"My net," Reg said. "The top and bottom are made from plastic irrigation pipe. The net is all sorts of things—willow branches, rope, whatever I can use. It gets torn up pretty often, especially by the high water. You two nearly blazed straight through it. If you hadn't snagged yourself on the pipe, you would have. It's the only really strong part."

He turned, looked Tom in the eye, and grinned inside his beard. "Almost stopped a small cow once, and I have to say I was pretty disappointed when all that beef slipped over the falls." Reg reached down and slapped his lean belly. "There would be more of me inside this skin if the net had held.

"The cans are to let me know if something big is

stuck, but they usually just rattle when the water is high, and I can already see that for myself. They gave out quite the clatter when you hit, and I still wouldn't have noticed if I hadn't been close already."

"You have rope?" Tom asked. Reg looked at him and winked. He tugged his braided beard.

"I grow it," he said. "The hair on my head doesn't work as well. Beard hair is thicker and has a higher tensile strength."

Tom stared at him.

Reg grinned. "It doesn't break as easily," he explained. "At least if I keep it oiled. If it dries out, it breaks right off, and I have to wind it pretty thin if I want to get any kind of length out of it." He turned back to the pool. "I use the net to collect things for my treasure room. So far I've only caught two people, and Argus is my first dog."

"You caught somebody else?" Tom asked. "What happened to him?"

Reg clicked his tongue. "Well, I'm not sure exactly. You'll see everything eventually. I'll give you the tour of all my chambers as soon as you like."

Tom stared at the frothing pool. None of this was really sinking in, but his body was still working, and he was still living inside it.

"What do you eat?" Tom asked. "Do you have anything?"

Reg laughed and turned away from the water.

"C'mon," he said. "I should have known. I'll get you something, and while we eat you can tell me your story."

He led Tom past the slick spot on the floor where he had done his coming back to life. The helmet and bag sat beside it. Tom picked them both up and followed the man and his dog. Argus seemed to have traded Tom for Reg. For a moment, Tom felt alone again watching the two of them together, watching Reg slap the wet dog's side, unable to stop smiling and muttering. It was odd to feel lonely when he had just found another person. But this man had been in here for three years and had found no way out. What could be lonelier than the prospect of a life underground?

I'm not going to live underground, Tom thought. I'm not going to stay here. If this guy Reg hasn't found a way out, he's either an idiot or some sort of wacko who didn't want to come back up in the first place.

There was a lot more to the room than Tom had first noticed. The floor, apart from cracks, was almost perfectly flat and smooth. The room was rectangular. The door to the waterfall was on one end, and there was another on the other side. Two more doors gaped black in one of the long walls, and the other, where Reg was leading him, was solid rock. The walls were almost entirely covered with carvings, some of animals and people and some in a sort of squashed-bug-looking language that he'd never seen before. A small stream ran along the base of the solid wall beneath a carving that looked like a lion with a curved horn.

Reg looked back over his shoulder at Tom and smiled.

"This is where I pasture my cattle," he said, and pointed. At his feet was a small pool.

Reg held his torch down close to the water, and Tom could see it was only a few inches deep. Round stones were scattered across the bottom. A wall of them divided the pool in half. Everywhere, there were small white creatures. Tom bent down. They looked like the crawfish Tom had occasionally caught in his stream, only these were bigger, and they were all white. They had a crawfish's thick tail that ended in a flipper, and there were two claws and long antennae.

"These are for eating," Reg said, gesturing to one side of the pool, "and these I'm either fattening up or saving for breeding."

Tom got down on his knees. There were hundreds of them.

"They're lobsters," he said. "Where did you get them?"

Reg laughed.

"They look like lobsters," he said. "I'm sure they're related somehow. They're crawdads. Some people call them crawfish."

"These are too big to be crawfish," Tom said. "I've caught crawfish before. And these are white."

"They're big because I only let the big ones breed, and they're white because they're albinos. Neither they nor their great-great-grandcrawdads have ever seen the sun."

Reg's torch sputtered and went out. The surface of the pool went black again.

"How many do you want to eat?" Reg asked. The unsteady light of the stone bowls flicked across the water.

"I don't know," Tom said. He turned his headlamp on and spotlit the water. "Oh, sick. What is that they're crawling on?"

"That right there," Reg said, pointing to a mass of black in the corner, "is a crow. And that over there is the last little bit of a kitten. I felt bad about the kitten, but the crawdads gotta eat."

"That's disgusting," Tom said. He was sure that he wouldn't be hungry anymore, but his stomach surprised him. Argus was sticking his nose in the water.

"Well," Reg said, "I figure that eating the crow or the kitten myself would be disgusting. This way I don't have to. The 'dads eat whatever dead stuff ends up in my net, and they turn it into fresh edible meat for me right on their fat little bodies. I don't have a fridge, so if the meat's alive it stays fresh longer."

Tom was absolutely transfixed. He didn't know it, but his lip was curling as he watched the miniature fat-tailed lobsters pick at the dead bird.

"Kill your light now," Reg said. "I've got plenty of stuff to burn. Batteries are as rare as stars in here."

Tom hesitated before he obeyed and then watched Reg wind some more white stuff around the end of his torch and relight it in one of the bowls.

"What is that?" he asked.

"A blend of whatever I find that will burn rubbed down in 'dad oil. This one looks like cotton mostly." Reg picked at it. "It was probably part of a T-shirt and maybe some towel. I get plenty of stuff in my net. I think a lot of people camp on this little ridge, and not a lot of them pack out their trash, judging from what I've seen. Of course, I don't really mind. The more that ends up in my net, the happier I am."

Reg lowered the torch back down to the pool. "Now pick the ones you want. Take as many as you like. It's your first day. We can work out a ration later. Figuring a ration for Argus will be a bit tougher."

Tom picked five, but Reg made him take two more. Then Reg took five and grabbed a few more for the dog. Tom offered to put his extra two back, but Reg said that he'd had a late breakfast and five was already more than he usually had at lunch. He was going to celebrate the coming of Tom and Argus. His community had tripled its membership.

Reg told Tom to set the crawdads on the floor, where Argus got a good look at them, and then he went and found a bowl and filled it in the waterfall because the crow was in the little stream.

"Wasn't the crow in the waterfall first?" Tom asked.

"Yeah, I know," Reg said. "Even worse, a cow is probably rotting upstream in it now, but it feels better anyway. If I was going to get sick from the water, I probably would have in my first week."

Reg threw all fifteen of the crawdads in the bowl and then led Tom through the door set in the end wall and into a smaller and much darker room. The only light came through the doorway behind them. Reg carried one of the firebowls in with two sticks and set it on the floor. He left again to set lids on all the lamps in the bigger room. Next, he set the bowl of crawdads onto the fire. It was smaller than the firebowl, and the flame licked up the shallow sides. He handed Tom one of the sticks.

"Knock them back in when they try to crawl out," he said, and sat down cross-legged beside the fire. Tom sat as well.

After a few moments of silence, beyond the occasional plink of a stick knocking a "'dad back in the drink," as Reg described it, the man leaned back on one hand and stared at Tom. He started to say something, then just stared. And then he swallowed hard. Tom tried not to stare back, but it was hard not to. Then Reg reached out and smacked Tom in the shoulder with his stick.

"Ow," Tom blurted, and Reg laughed.

"Sorry. I was just checking to see if you were real. I'd be lying if I didn't admit to having stranger dreams. You'd better hit me just in case."

Tom smiled and rubbed his shoulder.

"No, really," Reg said. "Pop me. I don't want to be boiling fifteen of my 'dads if there's just me to eat 'em."

"There's the dog," Tom said. Argus was lying down with his jaw on his paws, flame watching.

"That's right," Reg said. "Come here, Gus." The dog stood up, walked over, and began licking Reg's face. "The licking feels real enough." Reg pushed Argus down beside him and began rubbing his neck. "But you'd better give me a different kind of lick. I'd like to know for sure."

Reg seemed serious, but Tom was hesitant.

"Pull one from your pocket," Reg said. "You've got to have something in there, and bring it around hard."

Now Tom did stare, his mouth a little open. All sorts of memories were crowding through his mind.

Memories of standing in a mowed spot on the valley floor holding one of his first bats, with his dad pitching him slow balls. His first season of games in the city, with a small blue jersey and a too big hat. Standing over the plate and "Pull one from your pocket" coming from the stands behind the backstop. He'd never heard anyone else say that.

"Well?" Reg said. Tom leaned over and swung his stick at Reg's shoulder. He missed. The stick caught the man on the side of the neck. Reg toppled over sideways, yelping and laughing at the same time.

"Lord, help me!" he said. "I'm not dreaming." He sat back up, rubbing his neck, and reached with his stick to knock three scrambling crawdads back into the bowl.

"Now that I know I'm not making this all up, how about you tell me your story? Why did you come down here, and what went wrong? Assuming of course that something did go wrong. Maybe you meant to drown under the mountain."

Tom didn't feel like smiling, but he couldn't help it. He didn't really feel like talking either. He just wanted to think, and look around, and start climbing out of here. He did want to eat, even if eating meant the crow-and-kitten-fed crawdads that were still trying to climb into the fire.

"Where did you get this bowl?" Tom asked suddenly.

"It was down here," Reg said. "Actually, all of them were here. I've found a few cans full of coffee grounds floating in the water, but never anything like this. The stone bowls I use for lamps and burning, the metal ones I use for cooking. I have to be careful with the metal ones, though. They're pretty old and don't hold up as well as stone."

"Like antiques?" Tom asked.

"Maybe I shouldn't have said pretty old," Reg said. "Maybe I should have said ancient. They are really, really old. If we were back up top and we found one of these, it would be worth something. Down here, it's worth something too, but only because I can boil my meals in it. Actually, this whole place would make anybody famous who found it. There's a lot here that doesn't make any sense at all."

"So you're going to be famous, then?" Tom asked. "You were the one who found it."

"Well, I didn't exactly find it," Reg said. "Somebody else did. He was dead when I got here. I buried him in the cemetery room. I'll show you later. He was using these bowls. The hard part wasn't finding this place; that was an accident. The hard part is staying alive, wanting to stay alive when you can't get back out."

Reg's eyes glazed over a bit, like he was seeing things that weren't right in front of him. Then they fell back on Tom, and Reg seemed almost surprised to see him there, as if he were seeing him differently somehow. He blinked and shook his head slightly, his long beard braid bouncing around his chest as he did.

"I'm not telling you my story yet," he said. "We'll have plenty of time for that after we eat. You're new, and I want your story first."

Tom poked the bowl with his stick. "How long will this take to boil?" he asked.

"A while, and unfortunately the payoff isn't that great unless you're really hungry. But no distractions. Get down to it. Actually, hold on. Are you cold? You're still all wet."

"I think I've been wet for days," Tom said.

"That's a great way to begin a story, but wait." Reg jumped up and walked quickly, still limping slightly, into the other room. He came back with two stone bowls, set them by the wall, and lit them.

"Get your clothes off and we'll dry 'em." Tom pulled off his wet sweatshirt for the first time since he had put it on to sneak out his window. His jeans came off too. Reg draped them over a crooked stick frame and leaned it against the wall over the fire.

"Not great, but better than nothing," he said. "It

might get a little smoky in here—this room doesn't vent as well as the others—but the smoke makes it warmer. You'll get used to it. This is balmy compared to the winter." Then he sat back down. "Okay," he said. "Sorry for the interruption. You may begin."

"I don't know where to start," Tom said.

"According to some people, the beginning is a good place."

Tom puffed his cheeks. The beginning? His dad dying. Jeffrey Veatch chasing his mom. Refrigerator deliverymen. Packing foam.

"What's your name?" Reg prompted.

"I already told you."

"I know. I'm just trying to help you get started."

"My name is Tom, but my mom calls me Thomas sometimes."

"Hi, Tom. Welcome to the cave."

"Okay," Tom said. He wasn't used to telling stories. "So my mom got a new refrigerator, and it came in this big box."

"I'm right with you," Reg said. "It's been a while, but the last time I was around to witness a new refrigerator, it came in a big box. Go on."

"And this one came with a big piece of packing foam too. Anyway, my mom always thinks that I'll want to get inside the boxes and play and stuff."

Reg nodded. "Of course you would. Who wouldn't? If I had a big box here, I would be playing inside it right now."

"I think they're starting to die," Tom said, jabbing at the bowl. There were little bubbles coming up now, like the fizz in a soda.

"Good," Reg said. "Now back to the business with the box."

"I knocked the box off a rock, and the foam flew out, and some plastic. My mom made me go try to find them, but I couldn't find the plastic."

"I probably have it around here somewhere," Reg said.

"Probably," Tom said. He smiled. "She thought a duck would choke on it. Anyway, I found the packing foam, and it ended up in a creek."

"You mean you put it in a creek."

"I left it on the bank. Then there was this guy named Jeffrey coming to our house, and he wanted to play with me or something. He doesn't matter. Anyway, I went back that night because I couldn't sleep, and I floated around on the packing foam in the creek."

"Good man," Reg said. "That's why they make it."

Tom laughed again, even though it hurt his empty stomach. Then he described his descent into the mountain, his arrival at the beach, and the coming of Argus and high water.

"Huh," Reg said. "Argus was already down there at the lake?"

"I guess."

"I haven't seen him since I came down here. I left him above ground."

Reg turned to the dog. "Were you looking for me? You're a good dog. It took you three years, but you did it."

He rubbed the dog hard, and Argus rolled over, once again offering his belly.

"I was glad when he came," Tom said. "Even though he kept chewing on the body."

Reg looked up. "The body? What body?"

"Oh yeah," Tom said. He grimaced. "When I got to the lake, I found a body. I can't believe I forgot that part. His head was bloody even though he had a helmet on. He had a beard all crusted over his neck. I took his bag and his helmet. The bag had a couple batteries in it, a little knife, and some sardines."

"Sardines? Do you still have them?" Reg asked.

"No. I ate most of them, and Argus ate the rest. And I took a ring off the man's hand to give to the police when I get out so they might be able to identify him."

"That's a pretty good haul," Reg said. "Batteries,

a headlamp, a knife, sardines, and a ring. Can I see the ring?"

"It's in my pants pocket." Tom looked over at his pants where they were hanging over the firebowls.

"Don't worry about it. I'll see it later," Reg said. "Anything else?"

"Well, I wrote a note on the dead guy's boot and pushed him back into the lake."

"Did you really?"

Tom nodded, and Reg started laughing. "Well," he said. "What would Robinson Crusoe have done? I don't think anyone would blame you. I certainly don't. How anyone could ever get to us with all the water in these caves, I can't imagine. But it's nice to think they might be looking. That's more hope than I've ever had."

The bowl in front of them was now boiling happily. The two of them stared at it for a little while.

"I don't have any salt or butter," Reg said. "So start imagining whatever flavor you want to taste." He laughed. "I do have something else. I've been saving it for no particular reason, and it would be silly not to use it now." He hopped up and wandered into the dark. When he came back, he was holding a small box.

"Look at this," he said, and set it down. "This sort of thing is pretty rare down here. I've had the occasional soda, but this was a first."

What had looked like one box was actually a pack of four box drinks. Reg sighed deeply. "Just think, we could have marinated the 'dads in artificial flavoring. We'll just have to settle for drinking the stuff."

Tom couldn't believe how happy he was to see the small drinks. Reg broke one off from the pack.

"Crazy Berry," he said, and he handed it to Tom. Then they fished out the crawdads and set them steaming on the rock. When they were cool enough to handle, Reg showed Tom how to pop the shells open, suck the meat out of the claws, and tear the tail meat out all in one piece. The legs and remainders were thrown onto a pile in front of Argus.

The two of them sat, one broad-shouldered, pirate-looking man in his shorts and one skinny boy in his underwear, gnawing at the rubbery meat and sipping bright red juice out of jointed straws. Tom's stomach welcomed the combination without complaint and even with great rejoicing. To Reg, it tasted no different than it had every other meal, but it affected him differently eaten among other living creatures—one boy and one old friend of a dog. There would be no more talking to himself and no more of the other, far-worse option—no more silence.

The two of them finished and leaned back contentedly around the barely flickering firebowl. Reg smiled.

"Your first meal," he said. "We'll sit for a minute,

and then I'll show you around your new home. Someday, when I have grown old and died and you have buried me in the cemetery room—I hope you won't feed me to the crawdads—then this will all be yours. It will belong to you and to whoever gets stuck in the net after you."

Reg laughed and looked at Tom. Tom wasn't smiling. His jaw was locked, and his face was relaxed, even to his eyelids.

"I'm sorry," Reg said, very serious. "I've been down here a long time and have only had my own perspective to think about. The idea of spending years down here must be pretty hard for you to swallow."

"I don't need to swallow it," Tom said, "because I'm not staying. I'm going home." He reset his jaw and waited for the adult talk. He was going to hear the explanation of how things really were and the need for eventual acceptance. He had heard it many times. He had heard it from teachers, from the pastor of the community church, and from the priest at the Catholic church. He'd even heard it from his mother, though only halfheartedly.

He didn't hear it from Reg.

"Okay," Reg said. "You go 'head and do that. If you don't mind, I'll come along with you. This place has lost its appeal for me. If you die trying, I'll die alongside you. It would be a nice change of pace from fire-light and pasty-looking crawdads. They won't keep feeding three of us anyway."

Reg picked up his box drink and gave it a long pull. All it did was burble and sputter. Tom picked up another one and handed it across.

Reg took it, then set it down.

"Crazy Berry," he said. "No, I think we should save these two. They would taste better in sunlight. We don't drink these until we're standing beside a barbecue cooking hot dogs made from chicken, beef, and pork parts and every other kind of animal that doesn't live in a cave. When that happens, we'll sip down some Crazy Berry. How's that sound?"

Tom was smiling.

"It sounds good," he said. "Where do we start?"

"Well, we have to wait first," Reg said. "The water's too high because of the storm."

"The storm?" Tom asked.

"Can't you hear it? Listen for a second. Feel the rock." The two of them sat perfectly still and listened. "There ya go," Reg finally said.

"I don't hear anything but the water."

"Lie down and put your ear on the floor."

Tom did. He lay there silently, not sure if Reg was about to start laughing at him, not sure what he was listening for. And then there it was. He couldn't tell if he'd heard it or if the rock had just barely vibrated.

"What is it?" he asked. He didn't sit up.

"Thunder," Reg said. "And a lot of it."

Hundreds of feet above the small feast, Elizabeth Hammond was standing at her window. Darkness hid the willows and the rain.

~ eight ~

INFESTATION

Phil Leiodes, rubbing his scruffy jaw and clutching a box wrapped in a peach pillowcase, picked his way through the deep puddles in the gravel lot behind the bowling alley. The morning sunlight played off the water in a way that almost stirred some sense of beauty within Phil. But he was too distracted by the worms and by trying to keep his shoes dry.

Why did worms do this to themselves? Thousands of them died every rainstorm, flocking to the puddles and drowning. Was it like moths to flame? Worms to puddles? How did they even manage? The parking lot was smashed-up asphalt and gravel. There couldn't be that many worms.

Phil was pretty sure that he'd seen bloated worms in puddles on brand-new asphalt parking lots with absolutely no access to the dirt below. In fact, he was pretty sure he'd seen a worm from his third-story apartment window swelling up and dying in a puddle on the second-story roof next door.

A small piece of wood held the metal door open a crack. Phil still banged on it before he walked in.

His eyes had some trouble adjusting, but he found his way down to the basement and the circle of chairs. The awkward rumble of a gutter ball filled the room, followed by the sound of a machine swooping down to reset pins that hadn't been touched.

Pook and Cy were already seated. They'd been whispering to each other when Phil came in but went quiet as he sat down. The stairs squealed and Lotus walked his enormous body into the room. Another gutter ball rolled across the ceiling as Lotus eased his body into a chair. He was breathing like there were cobwebs in his throat. Staring at Phil, he pulled a container of mints from a pocket in his shirt, shaking it before popping it open and placing three beneath his thick tongue.

"Phillip Leiodes," he said. "You're goin' to Hell. You robbed a widow."

Phil laughed. Lotus didn't.

"I can put it back later," Phil said. "She'll never notice."

Sirens and the twins walked in. All three sat down.

Lotus nodded. "Whatcha got for us?" he asked Phil.

Ignoring the sniggers, Phil pulled the peach pillow-case up from beneath his chair. He dumped the long wooden box onto his lap.

Phil took a deep breath. "I found this on the top shelf of her closet. It's mostly just random stuff of her husband's—football letter from high school, some pictures of Dad and Granddad, arrowheads and a little sea horse in an envelope, bars and a couple ribbons off his old navy uniform. There's a Silver Star and a Purple Heart that can't be his, at least I don't know what war it would have been in."

"Are we going through the family photos then?" Sirens asked. He lit a cigarette and blew smoke out his flared nostrils. He looked at Lotus. "I don't know why we let him back down here."

Phil tried to ignore the man and focused on Lotus.

"There's a bundle of letters from Elizabeth when he was on tour or in the fleet or whatever," Phil said. "Along with all the letters from his wife, I found two from a friend. They were beneath the lining in the bottom of the box. One is dated about ten years ago, and the other only a little more than three years ago. They're both from the same guy and they both reference the treasure."

Phil held up the two pieces of stationery and looked nervously around the room. Cy flipped his eye patch up onto his forehead and began rubbing his bad eye with his thumb. Pook and the twins sat perfectly still. Sirens crossed his legs and stared at the ceiling.

"Read them," Lotus said.

"Okay," Phil said. "This is the old one. It looks like it was sent from an old navy buddy aboard the USS *Lincoln*. The letterhead belongs to a Lieutenant R. Fisher."

Tedrick,

I received your letter last week and am thrilled that you are exploring alternative history. It's generally more enjoyable than the stuff you read in textbooks. The photos you sent were impressive. Carvings like that definitely don't have any right to be on our continent. Developed from the camera of a dead caver found drowned in a distant lake? Even better. How sure are you that he was inside your mountain? You said his Jeep was found on your neighbor's land, but that might not mean he was anywhere near your land. If he was with people, they may have moved it to protect whatever entrance they were using. Of course, it sounds like all the treasure hunters are convinced it's on your land. Get some nasty dogs or something. Elizabeth might like them better than all your local dunces tromping around with shovels.

The photo of the stairs was the most impressive to me, just because it could mean the whole mountain is tunneled. The fact that it's all underground makes me think it could be a tomb and also increases the chances that what was inside has been preserved. Of course, I've heard things like this before, both from my father and from the various history professors that I used to pester with pet theories. My father found something similar on one of his archaeological digs farther south. But it was all Welsh and Norse carvings. I sent the photos to him, but, not surprisingly, he pish-poshed the idea of the background carvings being Phoenician. He thinks it possible that Phoenicians were on this continent, but a colleague of his insists that some of the figures were much closer to an ancient Chinese than Phoenician. That, of course, would make the things inside your little mountain (if they are really there) much rarer and more unusual.

However, when I suggested the possibility of treasure to my father, he positively harrumphed. In his view, it's not likely that the photos are legit, and if they are, then it's even less likely that any treasure remains in the caves. If the cavers in the photos haven't come forward, it's because they have something to protect. Maybe they haven't found what they're looking for yet, or maybe they just want to avoid having to hand everything over to the government because of our lovely treasure laws.

Our cruise is nearing its end, and my time in the navy is nearing its end as well. I'll look you up when I'm in civilian clothes again, you can loan me a headlamp, and we'll make you a rich man—if your lovely bride will allow such childish behavior. She will discover your hobby sometime, you know. Secrets don't keep, murder will out, et cetera. Regardless, pass my halloos to her and pinch the child.

R.U.F.

Phil lowered the letter and looked around the room.

"She doesn't know," Cy said. "She doesn't know anything."

"She didn't then," Lotus said. "She might now. The letter is ten years old."

"So Ted was interested that long ago," Pook said. "I thought he was always a denier."

"He was a denier to us," Lotus said. He licked his lips and then wiped them on his sleeve. "He never let us set foot on his land. He and Nestor both."

"What about the Chinese thing?" Cy asked. He slid his eye patch back in place. "We never heard it might be Chinese."

"Gold is gold," one of the twins said. "Treasure is treasure. I don't care who left it there." The other one nodded.

"Well, what about the part where he said there wasn't any treasure?" Sirens asked. "I'd hate to waste as many years as we have and come up with nothing more than carvings. What if those cavers cleaned it out?"

The twins began laughing. Phil smiled. Sirens bit his lip in irritation, glaring at him.

"*We* were the cavers," Lotus said. "And we didn't clean it out. All we found were stairs and a chamber full of carvings. The stairs out had been blocked off by a collapse. Stuff went wrong when the storm hit. They found Jerry and his camera in some lake and developed the pictures he'd taken. The cops published the pictures to get someone to come forward and ID him."

"Why didn't you?" Sirens asked.

"Questions," Lotus said. "We didn't want a treasure buzz and every chump in the county scrambling in our caves."

"You still got the chumps," Phil laughed. "At least until old Nestor started shooting at them."

"Why didn't I know this?" Sirens asked.

"Why do we call you *Sirens*, Roger?" Lotus asked.

"You never told me because I'm a cop?" Sirens flushed red.

Lotus shrugged.

"We're telling you now," he said.

Phil laughed. He was growing more confident.

"Do you want to hear the other letter or not?" he asked. "It's from the same guy and more recent. He became a professor."

The second letter was on very different stationery. It was dated just three and a half years before, and the letterhead belonged to the Department of History, University of Pennsylvania, Assistant Professor Reginald U. Fisher, Ph.D.

Theodoris,

I'm surprised that you wrote me, as most people enjoy telephones, but then you likely tried to phone and found that my number was disconnected. When I had a phone number that worked, students called it.

You find me at an excellent time. It is, as you say, the middle of the school year, but I have recently discovered that I am no longer required at this reputable institution (the chumps fired me). There have been certain disputes between myself and my superiors stemming from some of my more unorthodox views on early American history. (Having my father for a father can get you a job teaching, but it can't keep it for you. That's why he's stuck at the Smithsonian and can't get out. They want his theories in a basement where they belong and not in front of a classroom.) Of course, I can't blame it all on historical theory. There have been other disagreements about my theories on how history should be taught to eighteen-year-old lumps, and apparently some rumor has gone around that I assign grades to freshman papers without ever actually reading them. It's difficult to trace rumors, but that one may have come from one particular incident when I said as much in front of a crowded lecture hall full of students.

Of course, I am digressing, and I only have so much of this stationery left (I did sneak a whole stack from the department). The long and the short of it is that I am thrilled that you have made as much progress on your historical mountain research as you have. The cavers from those old photos found nothing? It's hard to believe that anyone could have hunted for that many years and drawn blanks, but if they are, as you say, a bunch of goons smoking in the basement of a bowling alley, then everything explains itself. I think that I am far more cut out for practical history, and as you have already done the difficult work (an entrance under your own nose the whole time? Are you joking?) and have seen stone stairs with your own eyes, then I shall gladly come along and reap the rewards.

By the time you receive this, I shall have moved out of my apartment, thrown most of my things in a Dumpster, and Argus and I shall be awaiting your arrival. Fly one of your crop dusters down (if you have a two-seater), put your old navy wings to work, and

take me home to surprise the wife. I'll be
waiting.

Best,
Dr. Reg
Former Assistant Professor
Department of Veneer History
University of Underappreciation

When Phil finished, everyone looked at Lotus.

"He had an entrance?" Pook asked.

"Seems like it," Lotus said. "Makes sense."

"Did I miss something?" Cy asked. "Does the wife
know or not?"

"We'll find out," Lotus said. He turned to Phil. "Get
Mrs. Hammond her box back. We need her trusting
you now. At least for a little while."

The men began shifting in their seats. Pook cleared
his throat. "You'll want to see the news tonight," he said.
"My brother in the state patrol called. Somebody found
a dead guy getting eaten by crabs on a beach. Big guy
with a bushy beard in a jumpsuit. It has to be Jeb. He
didn't leave town. He went into the caves by himself."

Elizabeth wound her hair into a pile on the top of her
head, trying to ignore Jeffrey. He sat on the couch,
nervously tugging at the skin under his chin.

"I'm going to walk down the valley to Nestor's again." She walked to the door and pulled on tall rubber boots before finally looking at him. "I'd appreciate it if you'd leave."

"Elizabeth!" Jeffrey stood up and brought his tall body closer to hers. "I'm worried about you. I don't want to leave you alone another night." Jeffrey shut his eyes and bent slowly, his lips parted.

"God in Heaven, Jeffrey Veatch!" Elizabeth arched over backward and pushed Jeffrey in the chest. "If you so much as try and kiss me, I'll use an eye gouge."

Jeffrey stepped back and then chuckled. "Eye gouge?" He shook his head slowly. "I've taken aikido, Elizabeth." He lifted his hand in a chop and placed it on the bridge of his nose. "It's a basic block."

"Jeffrey," Elizabeth said. "The first time you turned up on my doorstep, you should never have come inside. But once you did, there should never have been a second time. Now I'm going, and I'd rather not see you here again."

She reached out and patted Jeffrey's little belly before walking to the door.

Jeffrey plopped back onto the couch and put his head in his hands. He didn't look up.

Guilt had never been kind to Elizabeth. She turned around.

"Jeffrey," she said. "I'm sorry. I don't mean to hurt you. This has been my fault. That doesn't change what I said about you leaving, but you shouldn't blame yourself for anything."

"Oh, I don't," he said, waving his hand. "I appreciate that, Elizabeth. I know you're emotional right now. You need a little ballast." He started to stand up.

Elizabeth looked in his eyes. "Jeffrey," she said. "I don't want to be nasty. So let's just leave things right where they were. I'm going now."

She turned back toward the door, but this time the phone rang.

"Don't answer it," she said. But Jeffrey did anyway.

"Hammond house," he said. "Yes, she is. She's right here."

Elizabeth took the phone and stuck it on her ear.

"This is Elizabeth."

"Mrs. Hammond?" It was a woman's voice. "I could lose my job for calling you this way, so I should make this quick. I work in a law enforcement office on the coast. We've just brought a man's body into the morgue, and it looks like someone wrote on his boot, tried to scratch a message. All the officials say it's inconclusive, and they don't even know where the body came from, so they weren't going to tell you."

"What did the message say?" Elizabeth asked.

"I've only seen the photos, but I can make out a *t* and an *m* and then the word *live*." The woman paused. "I think it may have said 'Tom alive.'"

"Tom alive?" Elizabeth asked. "You're sure? How long ago do they think this guy died?"

"I don't know. I really should go now, Mrs. Hammond."

"Thank you."

The anonymous woman hung up. Elizabeth held the phone to her ear until it complained. She didn't see Jeffrey. She didn't see anything around her. She put down the phone, walked to the door, and opened it. Then she saw the sunshine, and the green grass in the valley, and the wonderful willows. She heard every bird. The phone rang again.

"Hello?" she heard Jeffrey say. "Yes, she's right here."

Elizabeth turned around and mechanically walked back.

"This is Elizabeth." And then Phil's voice was in her ear.

"Mrs. Hammond? I hope I'm not bothering you. I've been thinking a lot about you and your son. Anyway, it just seems strange that no one is looking for him when you're so sure he's alive."

"Search-and-rescue says that there's not deep enough access on this side of the mountain." Elizabeth cleared her throat. "They've spent some time on the other side."

"That's what I wanted to talk to you about." Phil's voice was all sympathy. "I've been talking to some friends about it. They've done some caving around here, and they think there might be an entrance or two into the mountain on your property and on the old guy's."

"Are they treasure hunters?" Elizabeth asked. "I only remember the old treasure hunters doing any caving around here."

"I think they did a little of that. Anyway, they offered—and I'd like to help too—to start exploring some of the caves along the ridge to try to get in and maybe find your boy. I know it's probably a long shot, but we'd like to at least give it some effort. I feel bad we haven't offered before."

"Thank you for offering. I'll have to think about it," Elizabeth said.

"Please do. We're ready to come out anytime. There's a crew of us, and we could use your property as sort of a base camp. Oh, and one other thing. I came out by your house yesterday to talk to you about this. I peeked in, and there was this box that looked kind of personal just sitting there in the living room. I knew people had been coming around. I hope I wasn't imposing, but I grabbed it. I would have felt awful if I'd seen it and then it got swiped later. I should have left a note or something. I'll bring it up when we come to start looking."

"Okay," Elizabeth said. Phil's story didn't even almost work. So maybe he was a thief, but he was bringing the stuff back. And he was offering to look for Tom. Nobody was looking for Tom. Search-and-rescue said they were, but she knew they were only fishing for a body.

"Should we come up then?"

"Sure," Elizabeth said. Phil and some weirdos were better than nothing.

When the front door finally closed behind Elizabeth and she began to descend the stairs, Jeffrey flopped onto the couch, rubbing his eyes.

That's where he was when the group of men, led by Phil Leiodes, banged on the door and walked in.

~ nine ~

REGINALD SPINS HIS

Tom's jeans were tight on his legs. His sweatshirt, which had always been soft, felt scratchy on his skin. Tom was following Reg down a long corridor. After they had eaten, Reg had led him back to the main room and through a door across from the crawdad pool. Tom watched the lean man's limp as much as he did the stone walls around him. Argus trailed behind and sometimes between.

Tom held a torch because Reg wouldn't let him use the batteries.

"This," Reg said, sticking his torch through a low doorway, "is what I call my calendar room, or just 'the clock.'" He ducked and stepped through. Tom stepped after him. "The floor in here is stained very dark, and there were some pottery shards when I got here, so it may have held wine. My guess is that this whole network of rooms was once some sort of tomb or treasury. In the ancient world, the two things were pretty much the same."

Tom held his torch above his head. The room was much smaller than the other two, and the ceiling was lower. It was also broken and cracked, looming uncomfortably like it had frozen in midcollapse. "Where'd the wine go?" he asked. He lowered his torch and tried to look at the floor. The stains weren't purple, just dark splotches on the rock.

"Who knows?" Reg shrugged. The flickering light shrugged with him. "I wasn't the first one here. There could have been hundreds of people through here over the years. The wine would have been vinegar for centuries. Pots could have cracked and just broken. If there weren't stains, I'd say it could have all evaporated, but I don't really know how that works."

He crouched and rubbed his hand over the dark patches.

"You know, it could have been an embalming room for servants or companions. This could be blood." He glanced up at Tom and grinned. "I think you're a bad influence on me. My imagination is getting grisly. I used to only have happy thoughts."

Reg stood up and walked to a corner in the rear wall.

"Behold! My clock!" Reg spread his arms wide over an odd stack of things.

The corner itself had become a crack, leaving a gap barely big enough for two of Tom's fingers at the bottom but wide enough for his shoulders by the ceiling. He could hear water inside it. Against the rear wall, just beside the cracked corner, a large clay pot had been shimmed level with little flat rocks. A tripod of sticks supporting a coffee can full of water straddled the pot. A fourth stick had been split in half lengthwise and then hollowed out. It connected the can to the crack—one end was wedged into the crack, the other end balanced on the edge of the can. Water from the crack steadily trickled through it and into the can. Another stick just like it leaned against the can's side, below a notch in the rim, and ran down to the stone floor, draining the overflow.

There was a puncture in the bottom of the can. Water dripped through the puncture and into the big jar below. A string of beard hair ran up out of the jar's mouth and looped over a notch on one of the tripod's legs.

Tom peered into the jar and saw that the string was tied to a red plastic fishing bobber. The other end of the string was tied around a piece of pottery dangling above another smaller tripod with a rock balanced on top. On the floor beneath the rock sat a metal bowl like the one the crawdads had been boiled in.

"I've made a bunch of different versions," Reg said. "This one needs improvement, but I haven't gotten around to it yet."

"How does it work?" Tom asked.

"Well," Reg said, taking a deep breath. "I punched a small hole in the bottom of the coffee can and figured out exactly how much water leaked out per hour. My watch worked for the first few months I was in here, so I timed it with that. But it was still tough because the amount of water that leaks out depends on how much water is in the coffee can, because the water pressure varies. So I had to find a way to keep the can full. That way the water pressure would always be the same and the drip out the bottom wouldn't speed up or slow down. So I set it up in here next to the little crack of running water.

"I sharpened a rock and used it to hollow out small trenches from two halves of a long stick. I set one stick back in the crack. The water runs down it into the coffee can. Then I bent a little mouth in the top of the can to control where the overflow went when it filled up, and I set the other little trench to drain the water onto the floor and back into the crack. That kept the can full and gave me constant water pressure. I had a wood float in the jar until I found a fishing bobber. It has a homegrown string on it that loops over right there." Reg pointed at one of the tripod's legs. "And the string lowers that bit of pottery as the water level goes up. When twenty-four hours' worth of water is in the jar, the pottery bit rests on the edge of the rock and tips the rock off and gongs my clock."

Reg reached out and gently tapped the rock. It fell from its tripod and hit the metal bowl on the floor. The gong was much louder than Tom had expected. The stone walls sent the sound waves rocking around the room and then echoing out into the other chambers. The bowl tipped slowly from side to side with the rock clattering in its base. Reg carefully replaced the rock and then stood up.

"I had one that gonged every hour, but it really got on my nerves. With this one, I just have to dump the jar and set the rock back up once a day. I'm sure I lose a minute or two every morning, but it's neither here nor there to me. Here's where I mark the days."

Reg held the torch up, and Tom's mouth opened. The wall was covered with squares, just like a calendar, each one labeled with the name of a month and filled with smaller carved squares for the days. There were more than forty.

Reg tapped one and Tom squinted. It was labeled FEBRUARY. The little square Reg was pointing to was marked XXIX.

"Last year was a leap year," Reg said. When Tom looked confused, he said, "It's a twenty-nine. Roman numerals are easier to carve, which explains why the Romans used them so much. I tried to keep track of full moons for a while but just got badly muddled. I used a deep stagnant pool and tried to measure low and high tide. If I'd been patient enough, I think I could have done it." Then Reg laughed. "You think I'm nuts?" he asked. "*I* think I am. Come on. There's a lot more to show you."

Tom followed him back out, looking over his shoulder at the disappearing water clock.

"Did you make that up yourself?" he asked.

"The clock? No. They go way back. Who knows how far. Some guy in Alexandria did a bunch. Probably the same guy who invented the first automatic doors. He used steam pressure. I don't remember his name. All the Greek cities used to have big water clocks. Archimedes designed some too, but he worked with gears, and that stuff is beyond me." Reg turned and put his hand on Tom's shoulder. "I will now lead you to the ancient treasure room of Reginald Ulysses Fisher the Third. You will be searched afterward, so no stuffing pockets."

"Oh, that's right," Tom said. "You wanted to see the ring." Tom dug his free hand into his pocket and pulled out the dead man's ring. He held it up in the torchlight.

Reg reached out and took it. Tom watched his expression change as he looked at the seal and then inside the band.

"This ring belonged to a friend of mine," he said quietly. He glanced at Tom. Tom suddenly felt awkward.

"I only took it so the police could identify him. I wasn't trying to rob him." When Reg didn't say anything, Tom continued, "I'm sorry I pushed him into the water. I didn't know what else to do."

Reg smiled. "Don't worry yourself. You did nothing wrong. This didn't belong to the man you took it from. It was my friend's ring first, but he hasn't worn it in a while. He's been dead for years. Do you mind if I keep it for a little?"

"No," Tom said. "Of course not. You can keep it for as long as you want." Tom's eyes were wide, and Reg was staring straight into them. Reg blinked and then shook his head slightly.

"Treasure room and then the cemetery," he said. "And I should tell you a story."

The two of them left the calendar room and were once more in the corridor. Tom was relieved to be moving again. "I want to hear your story," he said to the man's back. "How'd you get down here? What went wrong and all that."

"You will," Reg said. They passed two doors that

had been sealed shut by shifting rock. Reg stopped in front of a third doorway. It also looked impassable.

"Now," he said, "you will see all the wealth I have in the world. No laughing."

On the left side of the doorway a cracked column stood nearly straight. The right side of the doorway and all the tons of rock behind it had shifted and collapsed, closing off the opening. Holding his torch out away from his dangling beard, Reg got down on his knees, accepted licks from a pleased Argus, and crawled into the small hole that was the only space remaining. Tom waited a moment and then followed. He wasn't as coordinated with his torch, and his face was uncomfortably hot when he stood up on the other side. Reg was waiting for him and had already lit two firebowls. It was a large room, which might have been why it had collapsed. The ceiling had tumbled to the floor in many places, and the wall to their left was the only one that was really still standing. But spread out in the low expanse was Reg's treasure, much of it sorted. There were milk jugs and trash bags, piles of sticks, cans, and paper sacks, and whole mounds of willow branches. Closest to the door was a pile of shriveled-up things that reminded Tom of brains.

"It's all trash," Tom said.

Reg sent his eyebrows up and wagged a finger. "That depends on whether or not it burns, floats, or can be eaten or used to tie things in place." He pointed to the brain pile. "That's mostly nasty little apples and plums that I've dried out. I don't know whose orchard they're from, but somebody needs to prune their stinking trees if they want to produce better fruit. I keep them back here because I don't like the smell. I still make myself eat as many of them as I can stand, boiled into mush or dry. I'm afraid my gums would recede up into my forehead from some sort of vitamin deficiency if I stop. The previous occupant hardly had any gums left."

Reg waved at the piles. "Most of this stuff isn't that useful, but what hasn't kept me alive has kept me sane. I've sorted it, dried it out, and tried to invent, design, and use whatever I can. I can almost always burn it. The man before me had already begun collecting, and some of this is his, but I collected a lot as well."

The lean man shifted on his bad leg. He looked around the room and then at Tom. "The truth is that I stopped rationing myself about five months ago. Now I generally burn when I need a light and live as comfortably as I can. Three years was about enough time to spend down here, and I knew that using it up would give me an excuse to float down a waterfall and try to hold my breath until the ocean."

Reg lifted the torch as high as he could, trying to spread out the light. "There's never been enough rope.

For all the trash people drop and forget, no one has shoved a couple hundred feet of rope down my hole, and the willow branches won't hold anything properly, so I just burn them now. I've burned six times that pile you see right there."

He pointed to a mound of branches taller than Tom.

"It stinks," Tom said.

"It's organic and it's wet, so it's rotting."

"No real treasure?" Tom asked.

"Well, you found a ring, didn't you?" Reg said. He cracked half a smile. "Crawl back through, and I'll show you the only room that really matters."

"The cemetery room?"

"Yes, sir."

"Aren't you going to tell me your story?"

"I'll tell you there."

The roof of the cemetery room had not collapsed, but it had been lower in the first place. A once-natural cave with uneven walls had been cut and shaped into a rectangle. It was not a large cavern but large enough to swallow the torchlight.

Reg pointed Tom to the wall beside the doorway. It was covered with a lengthy inscription in an angular script.

"Do you know what that says?" Tom asked.

"Nope. But I can bet that it's something about a

boat. I would say that the language is almost Phoenician, but it's more cuneiformish, sharp-edged. Regardless, it's strange. Some would call it an ancient, almost prehistoric Chinese. That would be even stranger."

"Why a boat?"

Reg moved his torch down the wall until it lit up a carving of small, sailed boats. They surrounded a larger ship in the center. Tom's torch flickered and went out. He was a little relieved. It had been more of a distraction than a help, and his face felt sunburned.

"Just walk close behind me," Reg said. "There are a few cracks in the floor but nothing dangerous."

Tom picked his way carefully across the rough floor, staying as close to Reg and the torchlight as he could. They stopped when Reg came to an alcove cut into the wall. He led Tom in, lit a waiting firebowl, and sat down. Tom looked around. The walls were covered in writing carved carefully into the stone. Some of it was the same ancient script, but most of it was English.

"Did you do this writing?" Tom asked. "What's it say?"

Reg nodded. "This is the chapel. It serves the cemetery, but then this whole mountain is really one large grave. My coffin is just a little roomier than most. Some of what I wrote is from King David's Psalms. 'Yea, though I walk through the valley of the shadow of death, I will fear no evil.'" He laughed. "And some of it describes pranks I pulled in high school that I wanted to claim, along with more serious biography, in case I died and this place was ever found."

Tom didn't say anything. He didn't realize that his mouth was hanging open. Reg saw his slack jaw and smiled.

"Tom," he said. "I've been wondering how much I should tell you, because I wasn't really sure. But the more I look at you, the more sure I am. You look like your mother, but you act just like your father, down to how you set your jaw at me when I made you angry talking about you living your life down here. And how your mouth is hanging open at me now. He used to do that in class."

Tom blinked and shut his mouth. "You knew my dad?"

Reg nodded. "I had trouble recognizing you. You would have been only four when I saw you last, but I knew your dad well. He was a great friend of mine, really the only great friend I had."

Tom's face went numb.

"How are you sure?" he asked. "I could look like anybody."

"He had a boy named Tom," Reg said. "His last name was Hammond." Reg smiled, but before Tom could respond, his face grew serious. He took one deep breath and said, "Tom, I buried your dad. I buried him on the other side of this room."

Tom blinked and then turned to stare through the room's darkness. Nothing was making sense.

"My dad was a pilot," he said.

"Yes," Reg said. "I know. We both were."

"He flew crop dusters and little charter planes for Pook's airfield. He flew me up to a big lake once way up in the mountains where he would drop the rich people at their cabins."

Reg nodded again.

"We landed on the water," Tom said, sure that it mattered somehow. "But you couldn't have buried him. He died in an explosion. He was taking an old plane up and something went wrong. It exploded and crashed into a fuel tank. They said he must have died instantly. They only found part of his hand."

It was Reg's turn to set his jaw. He leaned forward, and Tom was startled by the anger in his eyes.

"Is that what they said?" he asked Tom. "Is that what Elizabeth thinks?"

"Dad's boss at the airfield called her. She picked me up at school. That's what she said. We had a funeral, but there wasn't even a body to bury."

Reg stood up. "That's because I buried him." He didn't say anything else. He walked straight across the room and Tom followed him, nervous and confused, watching the smoke from Reg's torch curl off the low ceiling as they went. And then they were there, in another alcove cut into the wall across from the first one. Four long mounds of rock sat next to each other. Reg walked to the third one and held his torch out.

"This is your father's," he said.

Tom looked the rock mound up and down. Reg was holding the torch at the head, where the mound met the cavern wall. The shape of a tombstone had been cut into the stone, bordered with a clumsy braided design. A thick square cross had been cut in the center. Across the top was written THEODORE DOLIUS HAMMOND. Tom ran his fingers across it. Underneath his father's name something smaller had been etched. He looked closely and read out loud, "In the ground, the best seed is never wasted."

Tom sat on the stone floor. "I don't understand" was all he could say. Reg handed the ring back to Tom.

"It's from the Naval Academy," Reg said. "It's our class ring, and inside the band are the initials *TDH*. It's your father's ring. Put it on your finger."

Tom felt it and rolled it over in his palm. He could barely make out the initials. It was big on his finger. He slid it on his thumb.

"Can you tell me what happened?" he asked. "Do you know?"

Reg filled his chest with air and blew it out between

his lips. "The story's a little long, but I'll tell it as best and as quick as I can. I'm sure you only care about the end. I was in the academy with your dad. We were assigned rooms together plebe year, we both rowed crew all four years, we both went to flight school. But your dad got out and came back here to get married and take over his dad's old place. I stayed in for a while.

"About ten years ago, a man with both caving and diving gear showed up dead in a lake quite a ways from here. Nobody knew who he was, but he had a camera and some car keys on him. The cops developed the film from the camera and released the photos.

"Some of the pictures showed men on stairs and in a chamber with inscriptions in the background. Then they found an abandoned Jeep, unregistered, on the other side of your dad's little mountain, near his property line. Your dad wrote me a letter to ask what I thought of the whole thing because he thought he might do a little exploring himself.

"All sorts of nuts came out of the woodwork and tried to get into the mountain off your dad's land, and that probably hasn't stopped yet. Not much more than three years ago your dad wrote me again. I had been out of the navy, gotten a degree in history and hated teaching, got fired even, and he asked me to come up to treasure hunt.

"You see, in his letter your dad told me that he had

found an entrance on his property that he thought might be *the* entrance and that he'd found stairs but wanted help. He never told me where it was. He just gloated cheerfully and said he wanted to see my face when he showed me. And he wanted someone to witness the expression on your mom's face when he showed her.

"Anyway, he bummed one of the crop dusters, picked me up on some patch-of-grass airfield with nothing but a ripped wind sock and an empty RV, and he brought me back. I didn't tell anyone I was going. I didn't think I needed to. Turns out we didn't ever get home. We went by his neighbor's place first, an old guy he wanted me to meet."

"Nestor," Tom said. "Nobody liked him but my dad."

"Right. Well, Nestor wasn't there, but your dad still wanted me to get the full tour, so we tromped up around this cliff to where he'd heard the treasure hunters entered. I think he wanted me to have the full picture so I could appreciate the entrance he'd found. We were both surprised when we found ropes and gear sitting around this little crack.

"Stupidly, we slid in and lowered ourselves through shafts until we hit a broken flight of stairs. They rose out of water up into the mountain. We climbed, and at the top the stairs ended in a small chamber. That's where we found them. Your dad knew all of them and let them know what he thought of treasure hunters trespassing on his neighbor's land. Apparently, one of them was that guy he worked for, a little guy. Ted quit right there on the spot and told them all they would be talking to the sheriff. There were a lot of them, and I was worried because they seemed pretty angry, but then they all got soft and started acting embarrassed. One end of the chamber had collapsed, and this big guy said that they had a guy who'd tried to squeeze through and was stuck. They wanted us to help get him out, and then they said they'd leave and never come back.

"Like an idiot, I walked right over to that wall and started poking my head through the holes." Reg stopped and swallowed. Tom saw his beard move and his eyes stare through three years' worth of darkness. "They'd been trying to blast through the rock. When they got us to walk over, they took off. Your dad realized what they were doing. He yelled and pulled me out. I remember being irritated when he thumped my head on a rock. Then, well, then the world ended. The detonation threw us both across the room together— with your dad on top of me—and then onto the stairs. I'm still deaf in one ear, but I should be dead.

"When I came to, my lamp was somehow still on, and my thighbone was pretty much useless. Your dad had taken the explosion for both of us. His right arm was gone just below the shoulder, his back was torn up, his legs were broken, and his scalp was split in more than one place. He was unconscious. He had already bled too much, but he was still breathing and had a real slow pulse. I got my belt off and cinched it around his arm to stop the blood. I was totally deaf then, bleeding out my ears, and I didn't hear the bastards coming back. I knew they were there when one of them kicked me in the head. I rolled over and watched this young guy rooting through your dad's pockets until he pulled out his truck keys.

"While I lay there, deaf and panting, this guy, holding your dad's keys, stared down at us. It was hard to stare back, straight into a headlamp, but I wanted to see his face. I'm never going to forget it—smug and young, black hair and a big jaw that I've broken in a lot of dreams. He was wearing a dirty tank top and had a tattoo of a dragon around his shoulders and chest. His lips were moving, so I know he was saying something, but the world was nothing but silence."

Tom couldn't take his eyes off Reg's face. Reg was having trouble looking back. He examined his torch, bit down on his lip, and glanced up at the ceiling. With a deep breath, he continued.

"This young guy reached back, and someone handed him a gun. That's when I realized how bad my leg was. I tried to crouch and lunge for him. I only hit him in the shins. He fell down, and I crawled on top of him. The gunshot made no noise at all. I saw the flame spurt out the barrel, and the bullet went through my shoulder. It only felt like someone had poked me with their finger. I hit the kid in the forehead with a rock, and he dropped the gun. I grabbed it and emptied it into the crowd of them while they tumbled down the stairs. The kid rolled out from under me and ran after them. I tried to sit for a while, waiting for them to come back. I blacked out. They didn't come back. At least if they had, I think I would be dead."

Tom couldn't breathe. He couldn't say anything.

"I killed one of them," Reg said. "I'd shot him through the throat. They just left him on the stairs to die. How long it took to get out of there is impossible to say because my headlamp broke, and darkness and pain always seem like forever. With my broken leg, I couldn't have gotten back out the way we'd come even if I'd been alone. I didn't even think of trying. I just dragged both of us away, as far away from where they'd been as I could, through the rubble and into the other half of the chamber that had been blown open.

"That side of the chamber just led to fast-running water—this whole mountain is running water. Your dad was dead before I rolled the two of us into it. It wasn't an escape attempt. I wasn't expecting to live. It was a long, horrible ride, and I held on to your dad the whole time. The water was low, and we ended up in the same pool you did. There was a little light there. One small firebowl flickering, and one old man dead beside it. I laid your father beside him against the wall of the cave, right where I first dumped you.

"For three or four days, until the place reeked of death, I slept beside the old man's crawdad pool, ate raw crawdads, and hopped around looking for more stuff that would burn. My thighbone had been snapped in thirds. I tried to set it myself and strapped sticks all around my leg to keep it from bending. I guess my leg is better than it could be, but it's not great. When it gets frigid in here, I have to use a crutch. I cauterized the bullet wound with the bottom of a metal bowl hot out of the fire." Reg ran his fingers over the round, bumpy scar from the burn just below his collarbone. He twisted and Tom saw a bigger, messier version on his shoulder blade, then he continued.

"Eventually, I found this room, the cemetery room. I brought them both in here. The old man had already buried someone, but he hadn't marked it. I buried him there." Reg moved his torch and pointed to the second mound in the row. Reg had carved a simple cross for his predecessor. THE OLD MAN WHO LEFT A LIGHT was all that was written on the wall.

"The big surprise was this guy." Reg pointed at the fourth mound. "He showed up almost two weeks later, bobbing in the pool. He'd obviously been in the water a long time. A rain must have washed him out."

Tom stood up and walked around to the other mound and another simple cross. MURDERER, it said. And beneath it, KILLED BY RUF.

Reg stepped beside him. "I would guess that your dad's boss decided to explain your dad's absence so that there wouldn't be a search. They probably drove his truck out to the airfield, put his arm in a plane, and blew it up. With that, they were in the clear. Nobody knew where I was. Your mom didn't even know your dad was bringing me up."

Tom didn't say anything. He just sniffed. Reg sat down beside him, but he didn't touch him.

"When can we try to get out?" Tom finally asked.

"First thing in the morning," Reg said. He looked at the boy carefully, watching his wet eyes in the orange light. "Tom. After three years down here, I've not learned too much. But one thing I do know is that our bellies aren't big enough for revenge. It turns sour and eats you up. We'll get out, but we'll get out for the sun, the moon, and mothers, not for small-souled enemies, though we'll deal with them when we get there."

Tom didn't leave the cemetery room for the rest of the day. Reg brought him a couple firebowls and part of an old towel for a pillow. Tom sat, stared at the carved tombstone, and spun his father's ring on his thumb. Before he slept, he stood up and carried the flame farther down the room, looking at the wall. There was another carved tombstone but no burial mound. It matched his father's, but the name on it was REGINALD ULYSSES FISHER, and below it was the smaller epitaph WILL GROW IN SUNLIGHT.

Eventually, Tom wadded the sour-smelling towel beneath his head and watched the firebowls burn down. Long after the willow wood and trash had become ash, the flames still licked around the stone bowl. Everything had been soaked in crawdad oil.

Tom dreamt of his mother. He saw her at another memorial service and beside another plaque low enough in the grass for the lawn mower to pass over. More pink and green mints. He didn't want her to eat those mints.

In the distance, and echoing through the caves, came the long, drunken morning gong of the metal bowl beneath the water clock. Tom, unaware that he had even slept, opened his eyes on darkness, but it was darkness with a story.

~ ten ~

DIVING FOR SUNSHINE

Tom stretched and yawned. His legs straightened and his toes bent backward. He had slept, and he had slept hard. His knuckles grazed a stone, and he sat up in the dark. His father was no more than a few feet away from him. But not really his father, just his father's body. Not even that. His father's bones, the bones that had held flesh, that had been used to lift his mother and walk and run; the teeth that had chewed, and the mouth that had laughed, those were all buried in this pile of rocks. But his father wasn't. His father was somewhere else. Caves and darkness can't hold you when you die, they can only hold your bones.

"Rise and shine, sunshine!" Reg's voice was distant but coming closer. Waking up without daylight could be depressing *above* ground. People got the mopes on rainy days. Waking up in a cave, in total darkness, with every cell in his pupils straining for the least bit of light because they didn't know better and he couldn't shut them off, with only crawdads in his belly and cold stone to sleep on, Tom was ready for a mound of stones to be erected over him. And Reg was yelling about sunshine.

"Sit tight!" Reg yelled. "I'm having some fire trouble."

Tom shut his eyes again, because when his eyes were shut, he could tell himself that there was light. He could see his house on the rock standing above the willows and lit by the sideways shine of a sunset. He could see his mom. She had her arms crossed and she was smiling, and for some reason her hair was blowing around her face. Why couldn't he feel the wind? And then he did. His skin felt a breeze, and goose bumps rose up all down his back.

"Here I am," Reg said, and Tom looked up into a torch. Tom stretched again and let out an involuntary gasp of air.

"Big day," Reg said. "I chipped it onto the calendar last night."

"We're going to get out today," Tom said through another yawn, still lying on his back.

"Well, I don't know about that," Reg said. "But something is going to happen, that's for sure. It depends on how bold we choose to be. We could get out, maybe, or we could die, or we could be badly injured going over a waterfall and end up on a gravel beach only to be found by a young boy who would carve messages onto our toes and shove us back out to sea. There are lots of possibilities, and I am happy with all of them."

"Do you like mornings?" Tom asked, leaning on his elbow.

"Not usually," Reg said. "I'm typically rather sullen over my breakfast, and I'm sure the crawdads notice. But what is truly strange is that I never liked mornings when I could have them with real sunrises and real dew on real roses and real paperboys wrecking real bicycles on the sidewalk outside my window. How I could ever have remained asleep and voluntarily missed a sunrise, I can't explain. If you're right and we get out, I don't think I'll miss another one."

Tom creaked his way to his feet.

"You're wearing a shirt," Tom said. "It's a girl's shirt."

Reg looked down. It *was* a girl's shirt, and it was very tight and very pink. There were two bubbly flowers around the equally bubbly text SUMMER GOD-GIRL across the chest.

"I don't know how anyone could stand to lose it," Reg said. "When we're out, I'll advertise it as having been found at the gates of Hell. Now come on. The water has dropped a little in the night. You've got to get something in your stomach, and then I'll fill you in on our options."

Tom followed him out of the cemetery. It was strange walking away from remains that he had never known existed, strange because it didn't really seem to matter. What had happened mattered; in some way, those bones mattered. But so did he, and he was still flesh, still breathing, a remnant of his father that could still affect the world. And like his father's bones, he was buried beneath a pile of rock, hidden from the sun.

Reg led him all the way to the crawdad pool, picked out a batch for breakfast, and began boiling them. Tom just stared at the sputtering torchlight, fingered the gold ring on his thumb, and shivered inside his sweatshirt.

"Argus is off snorting through my treasure room," Reg said. "But you and I have plans to discuss. Here are our options as far as I see them." Reg looked up from the firebowl. "Tom? Are you listening? We can try to go back in the direction that both of us came from. That would make the most sense in some ways. Tom?"

"Huh?"

"Are you tracking?" Reg whacked the first escaping 'dad back into the bowl. "But it doesn't make any real sense. The little pool you dropped into is fed by three separate small waterfalls. If we tried to climb up any one of them, we would be working against serious current at some near-vertical angles. I've tried all three and have never gotten more than ten or twelve feet up, and the water was much lower than it is now. I don't know how spawning salmon do it.

"We can try hopping over my net and going down the falls out of the pool. I've climbed that way before, and I've dropped a torch and counted to fifteen before it hit the water and went out. It would turn into a free fall at some point, but we could hope that the high water has made things deeper at the bottom. Hitting frothing water is better than hitting a slab-still pond. I'm willing, but only if you really want to. Your father died for me, and dying with you would be an honor, though not as great as dying to save you. Perhaps you could ride me down? But then you're not even listening, and I'm talking to myself."

Tom had his hands in the pouch of his sweatshirt and was staring into the firebowl.

"Where'd the spunk go?" Reg asked himself out loud. "I guess I shouldn't have to ask after what he learned last night." A crawdad escaped and died screaming silently in the flames of the firebowl.

"So Reginald," Reg asked himself, looking back to his breakfast, "what are our other options? Did you think that this boy would show up and options would just pop up where they haven't been for three years?"

Reg stuck his lip out and raised his eyebrows. Then he nodded. "I guess I did. I've explored every crack in every collapsed ceiling dozens of times."

"Reg," Tom said suddenly.

"Yeah?"

"I don't care about the treasure. I don't care if there is any, and I don't care if there isn't."

"You can't eat gold," Reg said. "But I will tell you something. If there is treasure somewhere in this mountain, then I would be happy to let it rest here for all time. And there are some people who could find it, and I would merely cheer enthusiastically and send them a well-chosen card expressing congratulations. But I would rather die than allow certain other people to find it. I would load it all in a dinghy and sail over that waterfall to Hell if I had to."

Tom cracked his first smile of the dark morning. "Do you think there is treasure?" he asked.

"Well," Reg said, "let me put it this way. Yes."

"Really?"

"I don't mean that I think there is a stack of Spanish gold or a chest of diamonds, but I think there is treasure here somewhere. How could there not be? We are surrounded by ruins, carvings, and pre-Columbian inscriptions; taken by themselves, those would be considered historically priceless. Someone made all this, and they made it for a reason. It obviously took a lot of time, and no doubt a few of the workmen were probably the first ones to float downstream and die. I don't think they would have gone to all the trouble of carving so many stairs and so many chambers unless they were hoping to fill them."

"But there wasn't really anything here," Tom said.

"Sure, but there were more chambers. The internal shape of the mountain has changed with the flooding of every major storm, and the earth's crust hasn't stopped grinding. Whole rooms have been washed away, flights of stairs gone. This could all just be a coat closet for something bigger and better."

"Do you really believe that?" Tom asked. Something told him Reg was trying to motivate him, to give him a goal.

"Maybe. I'm not sure. The crawdads are done."

While Tom ate, Reg said everything he had said about their options all over again. But he added a little more.

"So we climb and slip and hope the net catches us, or we jump the net and hope we land soft side down. I've clambered around in every reachable crack in the ceiling, and in some that weren't reachable, and they all go nowhere. Going the other direction is the passage that leads past the calendar room and the cemetery. Its floors and walls are near seamless, but then it was closed completely off in one massive collapse that

looks more like the work of an earthquake than anything else. The floor was snapped up and now blocks
the tunnel like a wall. There's a deep and rather narrow
pool that fills the crack in the floor right at the mon-
ster's base, and I've been down in it more times than I
can count. It doesn't seem to run anywhere except for
a little trickle off the surface. On the other side of that
slab, if there are more chambers that aren't completely
collapsed, then there might be treasure."

"So let's go that way," Tom said.

Reg laughed. "Sure," he said. "It will only take a few
minutes."

Tom stood up and hunted around for his bag and
helmet. Reg watched him, chewing on a final crawdad.
When Tom had slung his bag on his back and strapped
his helmet on, he looked back at Reg.

"I'm ready," he said. "Should we bring some food?"

Reg shook his head and stood up. He lit a torch and
walked into the corridor. Tom followed him. Reg
walked past the calendar room, whistled for Argus as
they passed the collapsed treasure room, and continued on past the door to the cemetery. Argus scrambled into Tom's legs and joined Reg at the front. The
passage narrowed, but the walls remained smooth.
Tom's eyes flitted from Reg and his torch to the walls.
At head height on both sides ran a single line of text.
Reg dragged his fingers along the left side.

"This is definitely the most similar to Phoenician. I've seen Phoenician script before, though I don't even almost understand it. There's a bunch of strange stuff too, things I know I've never seen anywhere."

Tom nearly collided with Reg when he stopped. He reached out and patted an enormous slab of rock.

"We're here," he said. "This is as far as this way leads."

Tom turned his headlamp on and looked at the rock. At its base sat a crack full of water, only about three feet wide. A trickle came in through the left wall, and the surface of the water rippled slowly into a gap on the right. There was a gap between the slab and the ceiling of the passage as well. Right at the top, a stair disappeared behind the ceiling. The ceiling had a network of cracks that ran back into the passage twenty or thirty feet, but none was more than a few inches wide.

"That's why I think this used to be the floor," Reg said. "That stair right there. The fact that the floor actually reared up means that there's a good chance that any chambers that existed on the other side might be nothing more than gravel pits now. But one hopes."

"So what do we do?" Tom asked. He had been sure, in surprising simplicity, that there would just be a way out, that Reg had overlooked something for three years and an old man for however long before that. A wave of dread drifted down from the ceiling and settled onto Tom. He felt cold. "This is it, isn't it?" he asked. "We really are stuck here, aren't we?"

"Well," Reg said, "yes. At least, I have always thought so. I'm willing to try the drop over the waterfall even though it would only take us deeper into the mountain if we did survive. But we should try everything else first. We beat our heads on this for a while. Then we try to climb up the chutes of water that filter through my net, and if we get nowhere, then we ride the falls."

Reg did not like how Tom's face was looking.

"Hold on, Tom. Let me be the hopeful one for a minute. Are you listening? Thomas, look at me." Tom blinked and obeyed. Reg pointed to the dark water at the base of the stone. "This crack is really deep," he said. "It's all split and uneven, and it narrows as it goes. I only fit in it for about fifteen feet. I've felt all over the face of the rock dozens of times, but it is dark. Maybe this is it. Maybe this will be the time I find a gap or hole that leads through to the other side."

Reg was trying to sound like he believed it. He scratched Argus behind the ear.

"You stay here and watch the hound for a minute." He pulled his pink shirt off with some difficulty. "And guard my shirt."

Tom took Reg's shirt in one hand and his torch in the other.

"Kill your light," Reg said. "We'll need the batteries. The torch is good enough."

Tom tucked the pink shirt under his arm and twisted off the lamp. In the torchlight, he watched the blotchy lump of scar tissue on Reg's shoulder blade as the lean man placed his palms on the slab and moved his toes to the edge.

"If I don't come up in about forty seconds, then hold the torch over the water." Reg was taking long, slow breaths. Argus was crunching on something. Tom was watching Reg's rib cage swell and contract.

"Why don't you take a light?" Tom asked.

Reg looked back over his shoulder. "I would," he said, grinning, "except fire doesn't work in water."

"Take the headlamp."

"The water would ruin it after a few seconds. We still need it."

"Put it in a plastic bag."

Reg cocked his head and turned to look at Tom. His eyebrows were up. He clicked his tongue against his teeth and shook his head.

"I have trash bags, but they're all black. It might glow, but it wouldn't show me much."

Tom dropped the pink shirt and slung his bag off. He had some trouble unzipping it with one hand holding the torch, but he managed. He pulled out the clear plastic bag, sealed shut around the two remaining batteries and the knife. Reg pushed off the rock and looked at the bag. Then he looked at the helmet and headlamp. Tom watched his eyes widen and narrow and widen again.

"This," he said, "this could work. I think it might." He grinned. Tom grinned right back.

After thirty minutes of difficult work using the dead man's little silver-handled knife, Reg managed to remove two screws from the back of the lamp and detached it from the helmet. It still worked. Then they sealed it into the plastic bag.

This time, the nervousness that Tom felt was more excitement than worry. Reg once more assumed his position, with a smudgy beam of light shining up at the ceiling from his right hand. He looked back over his shoulder, smiled, twitched his eyebrows, and jumped as high as he was able. With his hands still on the wall, he straightened his body and dropped into the center of the crack. Dark water surged up and around Tom's feet, soaking the pink shirt. He and Argus stared into the crack with wide eyes. The lamp glowed faintly and then was obscured by a shadow.

Tom started counting.

Reg was both surprised and frustrated. The water, dark under torchlight, was actually quite clear, but the narrowness of the crack made it impossible to see anything other than the rock immediately in front of his face. He spun himself until he was facedown. There wasn't enough room to kick, but he tried anyway, sanding his toe knuckles as he did. He pulled himself straight down until the crack was too narrow, and then he pulled himself along the bottom. He let bubbles come tumbling out of his mouth and relaxed, refusing to allow his lungs to inhale. They were starting to burn.

Tom reached forty. He wasn't sure if he was still supposed to, but he held the torch out over the surface of the water. He reached sixty. At seventy, he saw the light and a shape alongside it. He kept counting. At seventy-five, Reg's head burst out of the crack, gasping. He pulled himself up onto the rock and rolled onto his back with his chest heaving. He handed the Baggie to Tom.

"Turn it off," he said. Tom did and stood watching the water bead and run off Reg's oily beard and onto the floor.

A minute later, Reg was back on his feet.

"Anything?" Tom asked, but he already knew the answer. Reg shook his head and stepped back to the crack. Tom turned the headlamp on, gave it to Reg, and stepped away.

Reg was down eighty seconds the second time, but he didn't get out of the water after he had resurfaced.

When he had re-collected enough air, he pushed up and rocked over onto his side. The splash was large, and for a moment both his calves and feet were in the air. Argus barked in confusion, and then the feet were gone.

This time, Reg's body didn't get in the way of the light. Tom watched it fade slowly at his feet. It drifted to the right and disappeared beneath the wall of the passage.

There didn't seem to be more to the crack than he had been able to discover without a light, but seeing it made things different. Reg pulled himself along, as deep as he was able, down to where the crack narrowed and closed. The face of the rock seemed to have a bottom edge, a corner, but it was pinched against the other side. Only a few bulges and lumps kept the two sides separate at all.

Holding still and staring with eyes not designed to focus underwater, Reg could see where the crack reached its narrowest point. Where it wasn't closed completely, there was a gap, though it was only inches wide. The light wouldn't penetrate the water on the other side.

There was one bulge all the way at the end of the crack that hadn't survived impact. It had split off and slid down the face, closing the crack off completely beneath it. The piece was shaped like half of a teardrop, with its lump at the bottom and four feet of length ending in a sharp point for a tail.

Reg reached out and gripped the tail to pull himself along. The rock moved. He pulled again. It was loose. He tried to lever it away from the wall, and it stood up easily, wedged in the crack with its point aimed straight up. Reg grabbed hold with his right hand and braced his back against the sides. He pulled and pushed and swirled the stone, and the water was full of grinding. Then it slipped, the tail sliding easily through the skin of his palm, and a cloud of blood spread through the water. The stone dropped through the crack, into darkness, and disappeared.

Reg pulled himself straight down into the hole. His shoulders wouldn't fit. He extended his arms through, lighting the other side of the crack. He grabbed at the lip of the crack with his free hand and kicked his toes off the rock face.

Tom reached sixty. The light hadn't come back. The water was still dark when he reached eighty and one hundred.

"Reg!" he yelled, but his voice was tentative. "Reg!" he yelled, and this time he meant it. Argus barked.

❀   ❀   ❀

Reg swallowed water, spat, and gasped. He was on the other side. The pool was bigger here, much wider, and its sides were near-vertical rock. The ceiling was high and rough. This was a natural cavern.

Reg burst out laughing. Tom had been right. And he had brought a headlamp and a clear plastic bag. The climb out of the pool would be tough, and if they made it, the cavern might close off in another fifteen feet, but Reg didn't think so. The ceilings were too high. They would at least make a day of it.

Tom had stopped counting and was sitting beside the water. He wasn't even yelling anymore. Argus was drinking beside him. Then he stopped, pulled his tongue in, and put his ears up. He was staring down intently. There was the light. It was coming back up and growing brighter.

Tom stood. When Reg surfaced, he wasn't gasping for air, he was smiling. He pulled himself out of the water, stood beside Tom, and shook like a dog.

The pink shirt was lying in a puddle on the floor.

"I didn't give you that so that you could get it wet," he said. He took the torch from Tom and started down the passage.

"What?" Tom said. "Where are you going?"

Reg's hand was dripping blood, and Argus was

hopping around his wet legs trying to smell it. Tom hurried after him.

"Are you going to tell me or not? Am I going to have to swim down myself?"

"Oh, you're going to have to swim all right." Reg laughed. He turned around, black beard dripping, dark eyes wild in the torchlight, and he grinned at Tom. "I just thought we should bring the Crazy Berry."

~ eleven ~

CIRCUMSPECTED

Elizabeth slogged her way across a valley floor that was now more of a marsh, despite the hot sun above. By the time she reached the final bend in the valley and came onto Nestor's land, she had lost one rubber boot twice. The tall boots liked to stay behind when she lifted her legs. It was a small thing in comparison with her troubles, but it was enough to drive her mad. In sight of Nestor's house, she staggered for the final time and then stood still, with a boot halfway off, folded beneath her foot. She stuck out her lower lip, blew air up her nose, and pushed sweat-clumped hair off her forehead.

This was ridiculous. She was out of the house. She was in the air, smelling the earth and thinking of her son, but the earth wouldn't simply give off its aroma and let her think. It was joining in on the fun, the fun of making Elizabeth Hammond lost and helpless.

Elizabeth did what she should have done in the first place and what would have caused her to look sideways at Tom were he to do the same thing. She kicked and staggered around in the thick, squelching earth until both boots spun off her feet and bounced to a rubbery stop. Then she pulled off her socks, rolled up her pants, and stomped around in a circle. Somewhere inside herself, she wondered if her bare feet would find glass or a sharp stick, but the wet flesh of the valley came up between her toes and brought nothing sharp or pointy with it.

Elizabeth collected her boots, shoved her socks inside, and moved on.

Walking was much more pleasant.

She had meant to begin with Nestor's house, to be polite and ask if she could tromp on his land. She was drawn to the stream instead, and she walked along its bank. When she should have altered her course for the house, she hugged the waterline and followed it to the cliff. This is where the dog had gone down. It might be where Tom had gone down.

The moving water was hypnotic, a constant shape that wasn't really. While its surface seemed to hold its level, unchanging, it was moving, swelling and sinking fractions of an inch, a constant wave. Elizabeth watched the slow swirl of water rolling off the rock and down to Nestor's pond, and then she stepped in.

The sides of the stream were steep, and the water was still high. It was stronger than she had expected. One more step and she was in past her knees. For a moment, she wobbled; her feet slid in the amazing softness of the bottom; her arms waved, boots in hand; and then she held. She could see Tom now. She could see him with her shining unfocused eyes bobbing up, grabbing at the rock, and then going under. But she couldn't see him after. Had he scratched a message on a dead man's foot? Did he need help? Where was she while he turned white in the darkness and starved? How long before he surfaced on a beach somewhere?

She took one more step. She wasn't expecting her foot to find the bottom, and it didn't. The water swept her leg up, and she landed on her back. In less than a moment, the stream had gathered her weight and brought her body up to speed. She sputtered, and her face bobbed beneath the surface. And then something clamped onto her arm, something as rough as sandpaper and as painful. She let go of her boots. The rock tipped them; they filled and disappeared.

Nestor gripped a fistful of thistles with his right hand, and with his left he crushed Elizabeth Hammond's wrist. The water lapped around his thighs, pasting his denim overalls to his wiry old legs. Balancing and pulling and shifting, he managed to get Elizabeth turned around and on her own legs. She fell again, onto her face this time, and half the thistles tore. Then she was up again, and with Nestor behind her she reached dry ground and a group of barking dogs. She hadn't noticed the barking. She stood, with arms away from her body, dripping. Nestor staggered beside her. His cigarette was still burning, but he'd bitten and chewed it through. He spat it out in the grass and the golden retriever ate it.

"I'm sorry," Elizabeth said. She wasn't sure exactly what she was sorry for. Nestor wasn't saying anything. He was scraping tobacco off his tongue with his teeth. Then he looked at his sticker-filled palm.

"I wasn't trying to kill myself," she added.

Nestor looked up and snorted. And then Elizabeth laughed. His body had seemed large in overalls, but now, the way they clung to his legs, he looked like he was half chicken. His eyes glowered.

Elizabeth reeled in her laughter and grew serious.

"I really am sorry," she said. "Thank you. That could have been awful. It's much stronger than it looks."

"Can't do him no good that way," Nestor said, picking thistles out of his hand. He glanced up into her eyes. "What good are you dead? Dead stupid is just as gone as dead on purpose."

"I'm sorry."

"You said that already."

"I wish I could help him," Elizabeth said. She shook

her arms. "They found a drowned man on the coast. He may have drowned around here. There was a note on his boot."

Nestor raised his eyebrows and stuck his beard out. "What it say?"

"'Tom alive' or something like that. Nobody's looking for him. He's just stuck in there somewhere, still alive. At least until he's dead."

"Elizabeth Hammond," Nestor said, and his voice had trouble getting through his teeth. "I just made like a Boy Scout and caught you in time's nick. Now I think that gives me the right to talk straight. I've never been one for wives, not at all. But I always thought Ted Hammond had something when he married you. You didn't guff around like other women. When Ted died, I thought you might be the woman to handle it, to raise a boy to be like his dad. But now you got to find your handles, and you got to grip them tight. If your boy's alive, the last thing you should want to do is double his trouble. Don't try to run to him when he's in something thick unless you can bring him the answer."

"I know," Elizabeth said, and nodded. "I wasn't trying to."

"Mrs. Hammond, I'm not finished. If you raised your boy how you should've, then you know he's fighting with what he's got. If he dies, then you'll know he died trying, and that's as much as you can ask." Nestor clamped his jaw shut.

Elizabeth, dripping, stared at the water.

"I'm all Tom's got," she said. "Is he going to die wondering why I didn't come? Ted would have done something. He would have known what to do."

Nestor blew through his beard. "Ted's gone," he said. "But he left you a son made out of the same stuff he was, and don't you underestimate him. If you know Tom, then you'll have some faith in the boy. The odds might be long, but I'll bet on him."

Elizabeth looked at Nestor. She reached out and touched his arm.

"Ted always liked you," she said. "I know why. Thank you." She turned back to the water, distracted, watching it slide under the cliff. "But I still should have done something. I should have sent food," she said. "I should have at least floated a flashlight down there."

"You sent your boots," Nestor said. "And I sent a dog."

Elizabeth thought for a moment, looked down at her bare feet and back into the old man's eyes. She tried to smile. "Thanks again," she said. "Thanks for fishing me out. I'll see if I can't find my handles." She turned to begin her walk home.

"Hold up now," Nestor said. He bent over, popped a leech off of Elizabeth's ankle, and threw it in the grass. The golden retriever ate it.

"You're not hikin' back through the mud again. You just got it all washed off. You're gettin' a ride in Nestor's old chariot. Come on now."

He didn't wait for an answer. He turned and led the way.

Elizabeth, still very wet but dripping less, followed him to his ancient, once red, now pink, truck. The dogs all jumped in the back as Nestor pulled himself into the driver's seat. Elizabeth found her way around to the other door as the truck shook to a start. The sun had warmed the interior up to almost unbearable. The metal on the inside of the door nearly burned her arm. But she didn't roll her window down. While Nestor forced the gearshift into place and turned a slow circle in the driveway, she sat with her arms crossed and let the heat soak into her bones.

Elizabeth bounced on the split vinyl of the bench seat, and the dogs slid around the truck bed with an old tackle box. Nestor rolled his lower lip into his mouth and chewed on his beard.

"Whose rigs are those?" Nestor asked when the rock house came into view. Jeffrey's little car was still there, but so were three others.

"That's that Phil character's truck, isn't it?" Nestor sounded insulted. "What's he doin' here?"

"Oh, you're right," Elizabeth said. She had been just as confused about the cars. "Phil and some of his friends offered to help look for Tom."

"Yeah, they did," Nestor sneered. "Worthless treasure-huntin' buggers."

"Well, at least someone will be looking," Elizabeth said.

"Did you ask them onto your land?" Nestor asked. He kept his eyes straight ahead. "Ted wouldn't hold with them. Of course, they wouldn't hold with Ted neither. Free riches is all they're interested in."

"I don't know what you mean. Do you mean they still believe those old stories about the treasure inside the mountain?"

"I've said enough," Nestor said, and brought his truck to a quick stop. The dogs piled up against the rear window. "I don't like 'em. Ted didn't like 'em, and they didn't like Ted."

"Well, I don't have to like them, do I?" Elizabeth said. "If there were other men offering to help, then maybe I'd be choosy." She got out of the truck and swung the door shut on the seat belt. It bounced back open.

"Elizabeth," Nestor said. "If you need anything, you just holler. If you want real help, or if there's any trouble."

"Trouble? I thought I already had trouble."

Nestor ignored her tone. He nodded at the trucks and then up at her house. "Trouble," he said. "I'll come runnin'."

Elizabeth thanked him again and rattled the door shut, this time after moving the seat belt. Then she walked toward the stairs.

Nestor's truck didn't budge. She looked back over her shoulder at the old man. He was just sitting there watching her, like he was waiting for an ambush, for her visitors to come whooping down the stairs and grab her.

The dogs were all peering at her from around the cab. They started barking. She waved and then turned her bare feet up the stairs. She didn't look back again, but when she reached the top, she heard the gears grind and the truck start pushing its way back through the gravel.

Jeffrey was slumped on the couch, complaining and picking at his lips. Lotus had been trying to ignore him as he waded through the pile of papers on the coffee table, his bulk hunched on the edge of a small kitchen chair. His thick fingers weren't designed for sorting papers. One of the lank-haired twins was looking out the kitchen window down the valley. He was looking away from the long gravel road. Pook came down the hall with two shoe boxes full of papers and a small silver lockbox.

"This is it from the closet," Pook said.

Lotus nodded and looked at the guy in the kitchen.

"Anything yet?" he asked.

"Nope," the man said. "No sign of her. She probably got herself swallowed up by the mud."

"I don't think you're here to look for Tom," Jeffrey said. "You're not acting like it."

"Shut up, Veatch," Pook said.

The door opened and Elizabeth walked in. Her eyes went from Lotus to the coffee table with the shoe boxes and lockbox to Pook, who was chewing on his lip.

"Pook?" she asked. "What's going on?" Pook looked around for help. Lotus glared at the man in the kitchen, who shrugged.

Lotus heaved his large form up off the chair and turned to face Elizabeth. She stepped back. He was huge, and he seemed sick. She looked over his thick purple lips and his blotchy skin, then up into his small eyes.

"Mrs. Hammond, ma'am," he said. "My name is Louis Tuscanoli. Did Phil tell you we were coming? We offered to help look for your boy."

"Where's Phil?" she asked.

"He's on the mountain," Lotus said. "He and some others are looking for possible access points into the caves. You're all wet."

Elizabeth nodded. Her eyes went back to the coffee table covered with papers. "But what are you doing?"

Pook spoke up. "Elizabeth, you know I spent years working with Ted," he said. "He used to talk a lot about caves. He said he'd mapped some of them out. When Louis here told me that your son might still be alive, stuck in a cave somewhere, I remembered what Ted had said about caves on his land and thought our best bet might be finding that map."

Elizabeth still hadn't taken more than one step into the room. "Ted never talked about a map," she said. "He told me he'd found a way in, but I don't know that he ever mapped it."

"Well, we'll just keep looking, then," Lotus said. "If you remember anything, let us know."

"Those are just bills," she said, pointing to the shoe boxes. "And this is just old silver." She picked up the lockbox and walked through the silent looks that filled the room, down the hall, and into her bedroom. She didn't shut the door all the way and stood by the crack breathing slowly.

"You were making all that up about the map, weren't you?" It was Jeffrey's voice in a half whisper.

"Shut up, Veatch." That was Pook again. Then came Lotus's voice, far lower than the others'. She couldn't tell what he was saying.

"This is ridiculous," Jeffrey said, this time loud and clear. "You can stop pretending you're here for the boy. I'm going to talk to her."

"No, you're not." This time Elizabeth understood Lotus easily. "You're going to stay right there on that couch."

"What's your game, Veatch?" Pook asked. "You want us to believe you're the pure one? You're here for love?"

"Sit down, Jeffrey," Lotus said.

"Lotus." Pook's voice was almost inaudible. "This seems like a complete waste of time. We're looking through her bills. We've got a much better chance of getting something out of her than out of these shoe boxes."

Elizabeth had heard more than enough. She set the lockbox on the floor, took a few short breaths, swung her door open, and stepped into the hall. Voices went quiet as she walked into the living room. She smiled at Lotus.

"Any luck?" she asked on her way over to the phone. It was an old cordless and didn't usually work in her bedroom, but she was going to give it a try. She took it out of its cradle and turned to walk back to her room with it, acting as if she were dialing a number from memory. Then she put it to her ear. She even whistled as she walked down the hall.

Lotus nodded to the man in the kitchen. He pulled the cord out of the wall.

"Are you still going to pretend?" Jeffrey asked.

"Mr. Veatch," Lotus said. "What are we going to do with you? You're making a pest of yourself."

Elizabeth was standing in the hall with the phone and a confused expression on her face.

"The phone's not working," she said. "No dial tone." She walked back through the men and examined the phone's base. She looked from the unplugged cord to the man standing innocently in the kitchen. Then she plugged it back in. "That was easy enough."

"Elizabeth," Jeffrey said, standing up. "You want to run into town with me? I've got a few things I need to pick up. Do you fellas need us to grab anything?"

"We're fine," Lotus said. "What is it that you need?"

"I just want to get Elizabeth's mind off her troubles right now," Jeffrey said. "Maybe pick up some ice cream."

"Sure," Elizabeth said, and stepped toward the door.

"You know," Lotus said, standing. "Ice cream does sound good. But before you go, I'd like to talk to you, Mrs. Hammond. Do you mind?"

"Can it wait?" Elizabeth asked.

"I'd rather get it over with now."

"I'll be in the car," Jeffrey said, and stepped out the door. As the screen door swung shut, Elizabeth found herself propelled down the hall. Why didn't she just kick him and run? Why was she keeping up pretenses? Because if she did, then maybe they would. They would never let her go if they knew she was heading straight to the sheriff.

Lotus took her into the bedroom. She sat down on the bed, and he eased himself onto a small wooden chair against the wall. He pulled a cigarette out of his pocket and lit it.

"Do you need to smoke?" Elizabeth asked.

Lotus nodded. "Nice bed. Your husband build it?"

"No. It's been here since the house was built, as far as I know, and that's a long time." The bed was big, a king, built up from the floor and attached to the wall. Three of the corners had smooth posts; the two at the head held shelves between them. One of the posts at the foot was carved to look like the slender trunk of a tree.

"People don't build things like that anymore, do they?" Lotus said, exhaling.

"No. I guess they don't. What was it that you wanted to talk about, Mr. Tuscanoli?"

"Well," Lotus said, "there are a few things. Your boy. Caves. Ted."

"What about them?" Elizabeth was not liking this man's face. It was a face deciding what to say and how to say it, and the truth didn't look as if it was a factor in the decision making. And it was fleshy.

"I'm in a hard spot, Mrs. Hammond. I'm a straight shooter. I don't like to beat around the bush or leave people in the dark, so I'm just going to ask you a couple questions."

Lotus sat back and focused on his cigarette. Then he fished in his pocket and brought out his mints.

"You're not looking for Tom, are you?" Elizabeth wasn't really asking.

"Well." Lotus rolled his cigarette back and forth between his fingers. "Maybe we are. If he has found a way to the treasure, then we would very much like to find him. We do appreciate your invitation to use your property as a base camp. Hopefully, our search won't last more than a couple days. Afterward, if we've found anything, we will be able to leave town and your life can return to normal."

Lotus pulled on the cigarette long and hard, smoking it down to the butt. He blew a long stream of smoke toward the ceiling, filling the room with a haze.

"Mrs. Hammond, if you happen to remember anything, it could really speed up this process, and as I think it likely that your son was after the treasure, then the best way for us to find him is to find it. Don't you think?"

He pushed himself out of the chair, walked to the door, and turned around. Elizabeth still sat on the bed.

"For now," he said, "it might be best if you stayed in here. Jeffrey can go into town by himself." He dropped his cigarette butt on the floor and pulled the door shut behind him.

Before his heavy steps had reached the end of the hall, Elizabeth had opened her window. She would drop out behind the house and then make a break for Jeffrey's car, if he was still waiting. If he wasn't, then she would keep right on running for Nestor's.

She didn't even reach the stairs. When she rounded the corner and hurdled the lower chain, she came to a stop. Jeffrey was sprawled on the rock. The back of his head was resting in a small pool of blood. Pook and Phil were standing over him.

It took fifteen minutes, but Elizabeth ended up back in her bedroom. Only this time she wasn't sitting on her bed, she was lying on it, still in her wet clothes. Her ankles and wrists were tied together.

~ twelve ~

'DADS AND JAM

The bottom of the black trash bag was full of boiled crawdad dead. Those remaining in the pool wandered about, confused by the sudden spaciousness.

Reg had limped around for a while, feeling almost at a loss, like he was forgetting something, leaving something behind. But he really had nothing much to bring, at least beyond a bagful of crawdads. He held Tom's bag open and stared inside it. So far it held the little pocketknife, his two favorite sharp rocks, two box drinks, two old beer cans, and a small coil of black oily rope. He knew that this might only be a day trip. They might swim beneath the rock, climb out of the pool, and then hike until the ceiling slowly dropped down and dead-ended their journey. They might not need two days' worth of crawdads. But they would need fire still burning if they had to come back. He set Tom's bag next to the trash bag and began gathering firebowls.

Argus sniffed at the beer cans, then stuck his nose back into the plastic-wrapped pile of crawdads.

"What are you doing?" Tom asked.

"I want to make sure there will still be a light if we have to come back."

"Why would we come back? We can get past the rock."

"Yes," Reg said. "But we don't know how far past the rock we can get." He looked around, distracted. "I really need some rope. I've got maybe eight feet of beard rope, but it wouldn't hold either of us. Remind me to get some sturdy nylon rope when we get out of here. I'll always carry it with me. Do the batteries fit in the bag with the headlamp?"

Tom turned the headlamp on and held it up. The plastic bag was snug, but the spare batteries were in there.

After they made several trips to the treasure room, the firebowls were each mounded full. Reg dug around until he found an old coffee can and scooped a blob of something into each bowl.

"Crawdad oil," Reg said. "I skim it off the top of the water after each boil. It took a long time to collect this much."

Reg stirred the goop through each bowl and then set a stick bridge between each of them.

He lit the first bowl. "All right, Tom," he said, "we're off, and I do hope we won't be back." Tom picked up the bags, and he and Argus followed Reg through the room and down the passage to the narrow crack full of water.

"So how are we going to do this?" Tom asked. "Will Argus come?"

"Yes," Reg said. "But not on his own. We'll take the bags to the other side, and I'll come back for him."

Reg leaned the torch against the wall and took both bags in one hand. Smiling, he turned and stepped backward into the crack with his arms above his head. When the splash settled, Reg resurfaced, shook his beard, and reached out for the headlamp.

"Now you get in," Reg said. "Don't hurt yourself. Just sit down and scoot. Actually, get your sweatshirt off first. I don't want it getting caught on something."

Tom did and stuffed it in with the rocks and beer cans, surprised that it fit. He didn't want to scoot into the water. He put his palms on the rock the way he had seen Reg do it the first time. He gathered his breath and hopped in. He grinned at Reg when he popped back up, pretending that his back didn't hurt from sliding down the rock.

"Wipe your nose," Reg said. "Your lip's busy with your nose's business. Follow me down headfirst. I'll shove the bags through, and then I'll go. I'll pull you through from the other side if I need to. You ready?" Reg filled his lungs and pushed up in the water, ready to dive.

"Wait," Tom said. "Hold on just a sec." His heart was pounding. Nervousness was pressurizing his ears.

"Ready?" Reg asked. Tom nodded quickly. Reg surged again and rolled onto his side. Tom grabbed the rock and pushed himself down feetfirst. He could only see glowing bubbles and, barely, Reg's kicking feet, but he pulled himself around and tried to follow them. The feet stopped kicking and, after a moment, were gone. The light had gone with them. The water was black, but not for long. Tom blinked. The headlamp was right in his eyes, shining up through a narrow hole in the rock. Tom didn't think he would be able to fit, but there was Reg's face on the other side, blowing bubbles at him. Tom gripped the sides and tried to pull down, banging his elbows. Reg reached through and grabbed both of Tom's wrists in one hand. Trying to tuck his head when Reg pulled, Tom yelped out bubbles when his damaged scalp grazed the stone edge.

Tom opened his eyes and blinked and bubbled around a small chamber. The bottom was gravel where it wasn't cracked. The walls leaned in sharply until they met around the gap Tom had just been dragged through.

Reg had already grabbed the bags and was swimming off, wedging himself between the leaning wall and the floor. Tom followed as quickly as he could. Reg found the gap he was looking for, shoved the bags in first, and then twisted over and pulled himself through with his back dragging through the gravel. Little rocks kicked up and swirled, and then the light was gone as Reg moved into the next chamber.

Tom swam in the dark until once again he met the headlamp pointing back in his face. He really was uncomfortable now. He hadn't been underwater for much more than thirty seconds, but his lungs felt like they were bulging. Somewhere inside his head, panic was knocking at the door. He ignored it, relaxing his lungs and letting bubbles roll around his face. Then he twisted and pulled, sliding his own back in the gravel. From there, he only had to swim up, and he did, as quickly as he could.

When Reg returned for the dog, Argus was already paddling around in the crack. He tucked the dog under his arm, gripped Gus's mouth shut with his hand, and then made his first attempt. Argus wouldn't fit through the crack. On the second attempt, Reg went through feetfirst, pulling Argus behind him. The dog squirmed and kicked, but he came through.

Tom was still floating when Argus bobbed to the top and filled the cave with a strange yacking bark. Reg followed, spitting, with the lamp in his hand. The light gave Tom his first look at the cave and the steep walls surrounding the pool.

"Which way?" Tom asked between treading and spitting water. Reg pointed the light at the far end of the pool. The wall he lit up was just as tall and just as steep as the others, but it was rougher. Cracks and jagged rock covered its surface. Reg reached it first and stretched back to help Tom. Argus trailed slowly.

"You go ahead," Reg said. "I'll hold the light."

Tom felt around the surface until he found grips for both hands. Then he scrambled for a foothold. When his feet were braced inside a crack, he began climbing. The rock grew slick from his own dripping, though it wasn't as difficult as he had expected it to be when he had first seen it. He was still breathing heavily from his swim, but Tom made good time up the ten-foot rock face. As his feet gave him a final push and his head rose over the edge, his eyes collided with a wall of darkness. Tom couldn't tell if the cave went back three feet or three hundred. Tom hooked one leg over the edge and rolled up into nothingness.

"Tom!" Reg yelled. "You're going to have to catch the light. I can't climb with it and Argus."

Tom carefully eased his legs back over the edge and sat up. He looked down at Reg between his knees.

"You're going to throw it?" he asked.

"Yes. Are you ready? Catch it. You can't let it land on the rock."

"I'll try."

"Hold on, I'll throw the bags first." Reg set the headlamp on a little rock with the light pointing across the surface of the pool. Argus was paddling back and forth, looking for a place to stand. Watching him, Tom began to worry about how long the dog could keep swimming. Reg fished his beard rope out of the bag and zipped the bag back up. He grabbed on to the rock with one hand and leaned back. The bag sailed up and over Tom and rolled off into the outer darkness. The trash bag came next. It came shiny and dripping and disappeared against the dark surface of the cavern roof. When it landed, Tom laughed.

"What?" Reg asked. "Did it split?"

"I don't know," Tom said. "I can't see. It just sounded disgusting when it landed. It sounded just like a trash bag full of boiled crawdads."

"Check to see if it split."

"Throw me the light, and I'll tell you."

Tom leaned out over the edge with hands ready. Reg threw the lamp, and the cave swirled into dizziness. The light spun and twisted, flicking across the pool and walls as it went. The headlamp rose above the edge and slowed as gravity began to have its say. Tom stretched out his hands, but his eyes darted away from the lamp and around the cavern it briefly lit. That's when he saw the shape. There was something right next to him, long and low to the ground, crouching.

The lamp hit Tom's hand and fell. He wasn't watching. He was staring at a place in the darkness that he knew was filled by a creature larger than he was. Without thinking, he pushed his legs back against the rock and jumped, the beginnings of a yell stifled in his throat.

Reg was reaching out to catch the lamp, but Tom was coming right after it. He leaned into the rock face and let both the light and boy land in the water behind him.

Reg was somewhere between amused and frustrated. Tom's face, lit by the falling light, wide-eyed and widemouthed, had been amusing. But Argus was starting to whine, and Reg knew he needed to get him out of the water before he just stopped paddling and sank.

Reg took the beard rope and then felt around for

Argus. He thought he could find a jag of rock to tie the dog to. The splashing gasp for air told him that Tom had surfaced behind him.

"Reg," Tom whispered, and started coughing. "There's an animal." Tom was coughing, but he wouldn't stop trying to talk. "Up there. When the light came up, there was an animal."

Reg turned around. He couldn't see Tom, only a sort of disturbance in the water.

"Are you sure?" he asked.

"Yeah, it was right beside me, all hunkered down. That's why I jumped."

"I thought you fell."

"I jumped." Tom bumped into Reg. He had been swimming toward the man's voice.

"Stay right here. Hold Argus up if you have to."

Reg pushed out into the water and dove down. Below the surface, things were a little brighter. He was grateful the light had stayed on and the bag had remained sealed, or they would have lost it forever. As it was, he swam straight for the bright spot of light on the bottom of the pool. Near the bottom he hesitated. The light had settled onto a patch of gravel but was almost surrounded by a curving rock. The rock was black and looked like a head, a horse's head. Reg reached out, picked the light up, and ran his hand along the stone. It didn't look like any other carvings he had seen. It was broken off somewhere in the middle of the neck. The nose was chipped as well. The eyes were closed, and the stump of a horn stuck out from its forehead.

Reg flashed the light around the bottom, at the base of the rock face. He saw only one more piece of black stone, half buried in the gravel, and it looked like a leg. He turned and swam for Tom's legs. He could see that Tom was holding Argus, whose short legs were paddling in place.

"What are we going to do?" Tom whispered as soon as Reg surfaced. "We don't have any weapons. Just that little knife."

"I don't think we need them," Reg said. "And I don't think we need to whisper. Now climb back up there, and let's try this again before the batteries die."

"I wasn't imagining things."

"I don't think you were. Would you like me to go first? I don't mind."

"I don't think you should. I don't think either of us should."

Reg handed Tom the light and picked up the beard rope from the rock where he'd left it.

"I'll take Argus up first, then you throw the light to me."

Tom didn't say anything. He glanced up at the lip of the rock and then back at Reg. The man had already slung the rope around Gus's ribs and was cinching it tight behind the dog's front legs. Then he took the length of the remainder and tied the loose end back to the rope between Gus's shoulder blades. Finally, Reg put his arm through the loop and slung it over his head and shoulder. The dog was dangling on Reg's back, staring at Tom.

"Okay, light the cliff," Reg said. Tom did, and the man with his dog backpack began to climb. When he neared the top, Tom began whispering again.

"It was to the right of where you are. Be careful." But Reg either didn't hear or was ignoring him. He kept his eyes on the rock while Argus nervously pawed the air with his dripping legs. When he reached the top, Reg unslung Argus and set the dog on all fours. Then he turned back to the edge and leaned over.

"Okay, throw it."

"Is it there?" Tom asked. "Look to your left."

"Throw the light up, and I will."

Tom did what Reg had done, leaning back from the rock before tossing the lamp up. The cave spun again, but Reg leaned out and caught the lamp on its way back down. Then he stood up and pointed the light down for Tom.

"Aren't you going to even check?" Tom asked. "What are you doing?"

"I think we should see it together," Reg said. "Whatever it is."

Tom stared at the wet man with his tiny pink shirt and dripping black beard.

"I think you're nuts," Tom said. But he started climbing.

When he reached the top, he immediately looked to the darkness, but Reg was pointing the light the other way.

"Stand up, Tom," Reg said. "Are you ready?"

Tom stood and nodded. Reg pointed the light straight down at their feet and then brought it up slowly. It fell on the stone floor, then on a rectangular slab of black stone, and on that slab were two large paws. Between them was a head, and behind that was the great, carved, and somewhat stylized body of an enormous cat. Two tusks hung from its upper jaw.

"That," Reg said, "all by itself, should count as treasure."

"How did you know it wouldn't be real?"

"Because Argus was not barking or otherwise showing the sort of excitement he would have if a large animal had been anywhere near us, and second because there was a carved unicorn head on the bottom of the pool."

Tom looked at him. "You could have told me."

"I could have," Reg said. "But I didn't. Right now I'm wondering how many more of these there are." He had been holding the light low, spotlighting the cat, but then he raised it, and Tom stepped back.

The chamber had been partially natural but very much expanded. The ceiling was low and had crumbled in spots, but where it hadn't, column supports still stood. The floor sloped inconsistently where it had cracked and mounded up. At the far end it rose steeply and there were no statues at all. Every one of them had slid down or tumbled and broken. Where Tom and Reg stood, many still remained intact.

"What are they made of?" Tom asked.

"Rock," Reg said. "But that's not what matters. They're old, ancient even, and they're amazing."

Argus wandered off into the jumble of statues, and Reg stepped over to the cat to look more closely, running his hand along its head and neck.

"This is a tomb," he said. "Somebody's tomb."

"Why?"

"The animals are all sleeping, and they all have collars. They belonged to someone, or they're supposed to represent animals that belonged to someone, or just power. A lot of ancient tombs have had chambers like this, though not usually of animals. Sometimes real servants or soldiers or wives would be buried with the body of a great man, but in more civilized places statues were used. There's a place in China where an entire army of statues was buried. This is nothing to that, but it will still upset more than a few academic digestions."

"Why?" Tom asked. "Won't they be excited?"

"Yes, but also no. Lots of them will be. My father and his friends will be thrilled. I think anyone would be thrilled to find it, but not everyone will be thrilled that someone else has found it. Come on, though, we can't look at everything now. These batteries are due to die anytime, and we might have quite a ways to go still. We might still be going to a dead end and have to come all the way back."

But Reg didn't follow his own advice. He bent over, looking closely at the cat's stone collar. Then he laughed.

"What is it?" Tom asked.

"I think it's Asian," Reg said. "That would make it even worse. This looks like an Asian symbol, and there are Phoenician inscriptions in the chambers. I'm betting on Asians first and that Phoenician explorers left their marks later. A lot of academics would never admit that either group had been to this continent. Luckily, those ancient folks weren't able to read the academic journals or they might not have come, and there would have been no native cultures or civilizations in this part of the world."

"I don't get it," Tom said.

"You'll have plenty of time to. Just remember a few things and you'll be set. Columbus was the first to come from the east. Vikings don't count, and neither do all the people who were standing on the beaches and waving when he got here."

Reg was hunting around for the bags. He picked up the trash bag of crawdads and examined it.

"Stretched but not split," he announced.

"Where did the people come from?" Tom asked, picking up the other bag.

"Now you're catching on," Reg said. "A lot of people think they walked across a land bridge from Russia to Alaska, down through Canada, and all across the United States." He swung the light around the cavern. "But this sure isn't the work of a group of nomadic people."

"Where do you think they came from?" Tom asked.

Reg laughed. "In my humble and fired-former-history-professor opinion, they sailed. I think all sorts of ancient civilizations sent out explorers, and a lot of them probably touched down here. Some people may have walked over from Russia, but I'd bet my sack of crawdads that a lot of Native Americans descended from deteriorated and failed colonies established by ancient explorers who really did discover the place. Of course, experts will tell you that they couldn't have sailed that far."

"Why not?" Tom asked.

"Because they weren't us. Evolution has produced us more recently, and that makes us the smartest ever. After all, we invented the parking lot."

Reg turned his light back into the cavern and whistled for Argus. The dog popped out from behind a long reptilian creature. The loop of beard rope was still dangling off his side. While the dog stood there lolling his tongue happily, the light dimmed to orange. Reg muttered to himself and then sighed.

"Well, let's tromp on until it dies completely," he said. "We let ourselves get distracted. Of course, show me someone who wouldn't get distracted by all this, and if I had shoes I'd kick them in the shin."

"Why would someone want to be buried here?" Tom asked, hurrying to catch up to the now-orange light.

"Who knows?" Reg said. "Ancient pride? Take me to the ends of the earth. Wanted to avoid grave robbers for a few thousand more years. It would have been quite an effort. Big burial demands weren't uncommon. People following through on them after you were belly up and stuffed with straw was a little more unusual. Kings and pharaohs were generally smart enough to build their own tombs in advance. If they hadn't, more of them would have ended up in trash heaps."

Tom was having trouble listening, and he continually stumbled on the cracks and boulders on the floor. He couldn't keep his eyes on his feet or his ears on Reg. There were statues everywhere. A long-tailed bird was curled up beside him, and something that looked like a winged dog. He couldn't tell if it had scales. And there were bigger shapes off in the darkness, looming mounds with indistinguishable heads and limbs. They might even be on their sides, tipped and cracked by the shifting floor.

The chamber stretched on farther than Tom thought possible. The two of them walked while Reg talked and Argus explored, occasionally traveling with them and occasionally disappearing. In places, the floor was broken and they had to climb, once more throwing the bag of crawdads ahead of them and lifting Argus or pushing him up in front of them. The floor didn't always level out again. In some places, it stretched up, a long, slow, broken hill. In others, where the chamber narrowed or turned, it fell steeply.

After sliding down an uncomfortably long slope, Reg and Tom faced a steep climb. They stood in a junkyard of broken statues, breathing heavily. Reg, who had grown silent after the first hour, began climbing. His toes gripped the stone perfectly well, but Tom's water-squirting shoes slipped and slid with every step. His bare feet were badly blistered inside them. The light had dimmed much further, and when Reg finally turned around to watch Tom slide, the boy could stare straight into the dying bulb.

"Take them off if you have to," Reg said. "But get on up here. It's battery swap time."

Tom leaned forward and put his hands on the smooth rock. On all four limbs, he scrambled up twice as far as he slid down, made it to the top, and sat panting.

Reg handed him the headlamp.

"The honor is yours, friend," Reg said. "You've done it before, and I'm getting nervous. Maybe I'm just homesick."

Tom opened the plastic bag and looked at Reg.

"Why are you nervous?" he asked.

"Not sure really," Reg said. "I might just be worried that we're reaching the end of a tomb, the end opposite the entrance, but I don't think so. I think I'm just wondering how I would handle popping out into sunlight."

"What do you mean?"

"Right now, I believe that I would cry like a baby. You don't want that to be the first thing you see back on top."

Tom laughed. "I don't know. That could be neat."

He handed Reg the fresh batteries and then popped the lamp open. The light went off and the two of them sat listening to themselves breathe. Tom threw the old batteries down into the stone zoo and listened to them clatter. Argus started barking somewhere.

"Litterbug." Reg's voice came out of the darkness. "Never desecrate a tomb. You go get those right now or you'll rouse an ancient evil. Pack it in, pack it out."

Tom smiled. The first battery went in, and then the second. The light sprang back to life but not as brightly as they would have liked.

"That's not good," Reg said. "Those must have been used."

"They're not orange yet," Tom said.

"But they're awfully yellowy. White would have been better. We should go quickly while we can." Reg stood up. "Argus, they can't play with you! Come on!" He started whistling.

Tom was looking around with the light. They were near one wall of the chamber. It ran surprisingly straight given the state of the floor but still bulged in places.

"I think we should go this way," he said. "That dark spot might be a door."

Tom started walking, and Reg followed him, limping. His leg was working more than it had in three years and was starting to stiffen up. Argus stayed with him.

❁   ❁   ❁

Reaching the dark spot took longer than Tom had expected. The floor was badly broken, and the fresh light had made it seem closer. It was a doorway, a large doorway, and it held a thick timbered door. Reg pushed on it, sniffed it, and even gave it a lick.

"I wouldn't mind torching it no matter what's on the other side," he said. "But we don't have the appropriate technology."

"It feels really rotten," Tom said.

"It does, but it feels really thick, too."

There was an iron spike in the door that must have passed for a handle at one time. Reg pushed, pulled, and twisted it until he started to shine with sweat. Tom was looking around again, hoping for another door.

"See anything?" Reg asked.

"Maybe. I don't know."

Reg sat down to breathe. "Yell when you do."

There was another door, a much smaller one, but just as thick. Reg came when Tom called, and together they examined it. An equally useless iron spike was set in this one. Tom held the light while Reg threw himself against it. The door threw him right back. After several attempts, he switched shoulders. He was sweating hard.

Reg staggered back, slipped, and sat down.

"Reg?" Tom said. "Are you okay?"

Reg's eyes blinked, wobbled, and then rolled back in his head while he slumped to the floor.

"Reg!" Tom dropped to his knees, set the lamp on the floor, and rolled Reg onto his back. His beard was up on his face. Tom pushed it down and felt his neck for a pulse. His heart was beating.

Reg snored, a long, drawn-out snore. Then he opened his eyes and looked at Tom.

"You fainted," Tom said.

Reg coughed.

"No, I didn't," he said. "Women faint. People afraid of needles faint. Men black out."

"Well, you blacked out then."

"No, I didn't." Reg put his hand on his head. "We talked about this. I told you my leg hurt and that I was feeling light-headed, and we decided to rest awhile."

Tom couldn't tell if he was joking. "You banged into the door and fell down. Then your eyes rolled back in your head and you fainted. We didn't talk about resting."

"We should have." Reg smiled. He still hadn't tried to sit up. "Sorry, Tom. My body's a little pathetic. I've been feeling dizzy for a while, but I thought I could soldier through. I need to rest. The mummy isn't used to exercise." He shut his eyes and his mouth went slack.

"Are you asleep already?" Tom asked. Reg didn't answer.

Tom turned to the door, running his hand over the wood.

"Save the batteries," Reg murmured. Moments later, he was snoring.

Tom twisted the light off and sat down with his back to the door. This was not the time he wanted to rest, not right when they had found a door, two doors, and hadn't gotten them open.

Reg's snoring stopped. For a moment, Tom could hear Gus's claws scrambling on the stone floor. He must be climbing something, Tom thought. He whistled. Wherever Argus was, he ignored Tom. The snoring resumed.

After Tom sat in the dark for a few minutes, his impatience got the better of him. He had no idea how long Reg would sleep, and he didn't want to try and wake him because he was sure Reg needed it. He twisted the lamp on, unzipped the bag, and pulled out the little pocketknife. He flipped out the longest blade, looked at it, and then, kneeling beside the door, stabbed at the wood. The tip went in easily. He pushed a little harder, and then the knife folded, pinning his fingers between the handle and the blade.

Tom yelped and sucked the backs of his cut fingers. Then he straightened his knife back out. Even if it was thick, the rotten wood was extremely soft. He set the lamp on top of the bag, pointing at the door. Then, using both hands to guide the knife and being more conscious of his leverage, he made a long slice down the door, maybe half an inch deep. Then he angled the knife and did it again, right next to his first cut. He ran the blade through both cuts a few times, and then, wiggling and levering the knife, he pried out the pieces of wood between them.

Tom sat back and looked over his work. He had successfully cut an eighteen-inch-long gash into the door's surface. Cutting his way through the whole door seemed impossible, but that was because he couldn't think of wood as soft. He ran his finger through his handiwork, picking at the newly exposed wood. Bits came out under his fingernail.

He turned and looked back at Reg.

"It's something to do," Tom said out loud. "And it's not really wasting batteries. It might help." Then he went to work. Forgetting the snoring and forgetting the dog, he became absorbed in the wood and the knife.

When Reg woke, licked his dry lips, and sat up, Tom was still hunkered down against the door, scraping, stabbing, and prying in the headlamp's light. Reg stood up carefully, testing his leg.

"What are you doing?" he asked.

Tom spun around, startled. Then he scooted out of the way and pointed at the door.

Tom had started by cutting the edges of a square he thought would be wide enough for him to squeeze through. Then he had attacked everything inside it, trying to dig a hole in rotten wood with a tiny knife.

Reg limped over, bent down, and looked at it. As is the case with most holes, it grew narrower as it deepened. Tom had actually broken through to the other side, but the opening was just wide enough for two of Reg's fingers. He poked them through and pulled on the door. The wood around the hole cracked, but the door didn't move.

Reg looked back at the headlamp and the orange bulb, then he looked at Tom and raised his eyebrows.

"I thought it would go faster," Tom said.

"I told you to save the batteries." Reg stood up and sighed. "How long was the lamp on? Did you really think using the light up so you could whittle was a good idea?"

"I'm sorry," Tom said. "It was on as long as you were asleep."

"How long was that?" Reg was trying to keep the irritation out of his voice.

"I don't know," Tom said. "We didn't bring your water clock."

The two of them went silent. Reg was staring at Tom. Tom was looking at the door. Finally, Reg spoke.

"I'm sorry," he said. "If I weren't so feeble, this wouldn't have happened. I should have paced us better."

"I shouldn't—"

"Don't, Tom," Reg said. "Don't worry about it. It's my fault. We'll just have to do as much in the dark as we can. Pick up the light."

Tom grabbed the light and stood up. Reg positioned himself in front of the door, lifted his good leg, and set his foot against the wood just above Tom's hole.

"Okay," Reg said. "Turn the light off."

"What?"

"This might take a little while. I should do it in the dark."

Tom killed the light. "Don't kick the spike," he said.

When Reg kicked, a loud crack echoed through the caverns behind them. He kicked again, and Tom felt Argus come up beside him. He dropped down to keep the dog from getting in Reg's way. Tom heard the wood crack.

"Did it break?" he asked.

"Nope," Reg said. "But it's popping. I'm going to have to go with the shoulder a bit, just to distribute the bruising."

Argus pulled away and wandered off in the dark. Tom sat still, listening to Reg grunt and pound his body on the door.

"Do you need me to take a turn?" Tom asked.

A sharp cracking and a yell rattled through the cave. Something slapped on stone.

"Light, please," Reg said.

The light revealed Reg lying on his back with his head in his hands. His leg was through the door.

"Your hole helped," he said. His foot had broken through just above it. Tom began pulling at the large chunks of splintered wood around Reg's ankle. His shin was bleeding. Reg watched, and Argus returned to lick his head.

Reg carefully retrieved his leg and stood up, puffing his cheeks in pain. Tom stepped aside and watched Reg tear into the door, peeling the old wood back a few more inches. Then, hands and head first, Reg fed himself through. Before Tom had time to move, Argus hopped through after him.

"Hand the light through," Reg said. Tom did and ducked to follow.

"Oh my," Tom heard, and then he stood up.

The room was not terribly large, though the ceilings were at least twenty feet high and, like some other parts of the caves, speckled with stalactites. One particularly large one dripped down over the platform that held the sarcophagus. Thick rectangular columns, no more than six feet tall, stood on each corner of the platform like the posts on a bed. Strangest of all, the room was full of jingling and plinking sounds, like a dining room busy with toasts.

"Over there." Reg pointed the light as if Tom had asked about the sound. A small line of water was trickling down the wall behind the platform. About four feet above the ground it entered a large round basin, which overflowed through two notches on either side. The basin was full of shining spheres, like blown-glass balls—not much bigger than baseballs—gently rolling and colliding where they floated.

The water that spilled from the basin fed into a narrow trough cut into the floor. It divided in two around the platform only to rejoin on the other side. The small stream exited the room under an enormous door, the same size as the first one Reg had banged on, except it wasn't made of wood. It was a solid slab of stone.

"That door probably leads to some sort of treasure room or at least a dead wife." Reg walked to the platform and stepped onto it. The sarcophagus was made of stone and was roughly the shape of a man, tapering at the legs, with enormously broad shoulders below a bulge of a head. But there wasn't an image of a man carved onto it. Instead, there was a network of small branches and leaves. At the chest, there was a single carved dove, curled up either in sleep or in death.

Above it, on a smooth circle free of leaves, was the same symbol that had been on the stone animals' collars.

"We should hurry," Reg said, looking up and around the room.

"There's another small door right there," Tom said. He had followed Reg to the dais but was pointing to the wall across from where they'd entered. He looked back down at the sarcophagus. "Who do you think this was?"

Reg looked at him and then walked over to the fountain. He picked up a sphere and held it up to the light.

"It can't be solid if it floats," he said. He rolled the sphere around his palm and found what he was looking for on one side of the ball, a slight lump where a blowing rod could have been broken off. He found the symbol they had seen on the sarcophagus cut, or maybe stamped, into the surface. "If we could read that, I'm pretty sure we'd know whose bedroom this is."

"The light is getting oranger," Tom said.

Reg nodded, set the ball back in the fountain, and he and Tom both walked quickly to the small doorway. Argus was drinking from the stream in the floor.

"Pray this isn't a broom closet," Reg said as he gripped the iron spike.

The door opened easily and Reg staggered back,

nearly falling in overbalanced surprise. The light staggered away with him. Tom bit his lip as he stared through the dark doorway, waiting for Reg to lift the light so that he could see. He knew there was not a lot of light left and they would be feeling their way along in the dark when the batteries died or they might have to return to Reg's caves in completely disorienting blackness.

Reg steadied himself and turned the light. Stone steps rose up from the floor in front of them.

They were long stairs, winding inconsistently, and hard on Tom's blisters and Reg's leg. In some places, they tipped or angled to the side. In more than a few spots a crack had cut completely across the tunnel, and the two halves had shifted in different directions, leaving an opening only inches wide. The tightest of these skinned Argus's sides as he was pushed and pulled through. A healthier Reg would never have fit. As it was, he writhed and squirmed, leaving behind strips of his pink T-shirt and skin from his chest and back. Eventually, all three of them and their sack of crawdads arrived at the top. The top was a wall of bricks of various sizes, all carved from the same black stone as the zoo down below.

Reg clicked his teeth loudly and looked at the wall in the slowly dying light.

"If you have to eat me, start with my bad leg," he said.

"I won't eat you."

"I was talking to Argus."

In the top row, one brick was missing. The hole was large enough for Reg's hand, and he worked his arm through, pushing and pulling at the edges of the hole. Old mortar ground slowly, and a brick slid. Reg dug through Tom's bag and pulled out one of his rocks. He shoved it into the gap and began banging slowly, using almost as much knuckle as rock. Finally, the brick dropped on the other side with a crunch. The two of them looked at each other.

"Was that breaking glass?" Reg asked. Tom nodded, and Reg got to work on the next one.

The hole gradually grew, and the small stairway filled with dust and coughing. Reg worked and sweated, and then Tom pulled and pushed until his fingers bled. Finally, in the last of the orange light, Reg boosted Tom, and the boy scrambled through and fell on the other side. He fell through things. He heard wood crack and more glass shatter. Glass dug into his shoulder. The light was passed through, and Tom looked around.

"I don't see a way out, but I think you'll like this" was all he would say. Working from both sides, they spread the hole farther down, and Argus was handed through. Then came a completely dust-coated Reg. He looked around and up and then smiled.

"We are in a storm cellar," he said. He looked at his bare and bloody feet. "And we broke some glass things." The light was almost completely dead, but they could barely make out dust-covered shelves lining the black brick walls, some collapsed and empty, some full. There was a silver teapot and what looked like a punch bowl. In the corner were two old muskets and a small keg, which Reg said was probably gunpowder. There were tins of food too rusted to think about, and there was a small oil lamp.

"Ah," Reg sighed. "I should have brought some 'dad oil. I knew I would forget something." He lifted the glass off the top and felt the wick. It was as dry as the mortar had been between the stones. Back behind it, hiding in brick-and-mortar wreckage, was a can. Reg pulled it out, sniffed it, and laughed. He filled the lamp with oil as quickly as he could and adjusted the wick.

"How are you going to light it?"

"Is it too much to ask?" Reg muttered. "All the gods, saints, and angels, it is a storm cellar."

The headlamp died completely and darkness descended, but Reg was laughing again. Tom could hear him fumbling with something.

"Please, God," Reg said, and struck a match.

Tom's eyes greeted Reg's through the tiny flame of

an antique match. Reg carefully kissed it to the lantern's wick, and the flame grew. His mouth spread wide, and he grinned at Tom. Then he looked at the ceiling. A ladder was against the wall, but the ceiling was made of heavy-looking beams. He climbed up and gave it one push. It didn't budge.

"Let's eat first," Reg said, and he stepped back down to root through the shelves. Tom kicked as much of the broken glass as he could back out of Reg's way and into a corner. There was nothing they dared touch but one lonely half-pint of jam older than Tom's great-grandfather. The two of them sat in the rubble with the lantern between them and dipped their crawdads in very old raspberry. After one trip back down the long stairs, Tom's legs ached and his feet were raw, but they also had beer cans full of water.

"You know," Reg said, "we're going to get out. We really are. Even if we have to set fire to the ceiling." He glopped jam onto a white crawdad tail with a grit-covered finger. "But we have to eat enough of this so that we get sick and die a couple days after."

~ thirteen ~

EASTER

Lotus was picking his teeth with his thumbnail. Sirens had just arrived. Cy, Phil, and the twins were searching the mountain.

"Let me get this straight," Sirens said. "She walked in while you and Pook were going through her bills, so now she's tied up in her room?" He raised his eyebrows and licked his lips. "You just cranked the stakes up a bit."

"I think, Sirens," Lotus said, wiping some plaque on the arm of the couch, "that you are overreacting."

"How's that?" Sirens asked. "She gives in or she dies. Am I missing something? Last time I checked, Jeffrey Veatch is tied up behind the couch bleeding on the floor. Are you thinking of going double homicide?"

"What's all this *you* business? You should be saying *we*, Sirens." Pook was pacing the floor by the couch. Lotus examined his thumb and then popped it back in his mouth. "You're in deep," Pook continued, "and judges hate crooked cops."

Sirens glared at Pook and then turned to Lotus.

The fat man smiled. "Pook," he said. "Why don't you go check in with our friends on the ridge while I speak with local law enforcement."

Pook stormed to the door, muttering, and slammed it behind him.

"You need cheering up, Sirens," Lotus said. "So I'll point out one important aspect of Mrs. Hammond's situation that you seem to be missing. She is a lonely woman dealing with grief and depression. She could easily be a danger to herself. Elizabeth Hammond might not be able to tell anyone her story after we leave."

Elizabeth's arms were falling asleep tied behind her back. She'd tried rolling onto her side, but her shoulder started to ache within minutes. Then she'd switched sides and let the other one throb for a while. She'd rolled onto her face, but that hadn't lasted long. She occasionally heard voices down the hall. At least two men had been having an argument in the living room, and she thought one or two others might be just behind the house on the ridge. By the time the bedroom door opened, she had managed to twist and shuffle herself onto her back, with the bedspread tangled up around her legs. She was breathing hard and trying not to scream. She was pretty sure that she could control herself if someone would just straighten her bedding back up and pull the little mounds flat.

"Mrs. Hammond, I'm really sorry about all this," Phil said. He stepped on Lotus's old cigarette butt and sat down in the same chair. Sweat was dripping off the tip of his nose and his tank top was sticking to him. His face was flushed, and the scar above his eye stood out like a fresh gash. She could see most of his tattoo now—a Chinese dragon clawing its way up his chest. "I don't know how this all happened."

"Did you bring my box back?" she asked.

"Actually, I did. Hold on." Phil hurried out of the room, leaving the door open. Elizabeth thrashed and tried to kick the bedspread flat. She only made it worse.

Phil walked back in and set the wooden box on the floor. Then he sat back down.

"I want to help you, Elizabeth," he said. "I don't care about treasure."

"Could you do something for me?" Elizabeth asked.

"Sure," he said.

"Could you go dial the sheriff and hold the phone to my ear?"

Phil tried to smile.

"I'm serious, Elizabeth," he said. "I'm not with them on this. I want to find your boy. I thought they did too, but they're more interested in their treasure hunt. You're kind of a problem for them now, Elizabeth. I don't want you to get hurt. I'm worried."

"I can tell," she said. "Very selfless of you. What are you hoping to do about your worries?"

Phil cleared his throat and looked down. "I want you to marry me, Elizabeth."

"*What?*"

"If I resign my share of whatever treasure is found and you marry me, then they'll call everything even. You live, and they get my portion. Of course, we would have to allow them access to our property and complete treasure rights."

Phil looked up and into Elizabeth's surprised eyes. "I'm not asking for an answer now. I'll go and keep hunting with the others for any caves, and I'll come back."

When the door shut, she made a face and then kicked wildly, flopping her body. Something popped loudly beneath her and she stopped. She had never thought it possible to break this bed. She'd even let Tom jump on it, at least when the sheets were being washed.

She took a deep breath and blew out slowly. She didn't believe Phil for an instant.

"Fake my suicide and you lose the land," Elizabeth said out loud. "Marry me and then fake my suicide and you can keep it legally. Is that the game, Phillip?"

✾   ✾   ✾

Phil walked into the living room and sat on the coffee table.

"How'd it go?" Lotus asked.

"I wouldn't say good," Phil said.

"Her feelings are otherwise engaged," a voice said from behind the couch.

"Is that you, Veatch?" Lotus asked. "You still alive?"

Sirens was sitting on the couch and wearing an extremely somber face. He stood and peeked over the back of the couch.

A white plastic bag had been placed under Jeffrey's head. It was no longer white and had scabbed to a mat of his hair.

"Untie me," Jeffrey said. "I want to talk to you."

"Pull him up, Phil," Lotus said. "If he gets boring, he can go right back."

Jeffrey was dragged out by his shoulders and then propped up with his back against the couch. The bag was still blood-glued to the back of his head and stood out around it like a white plastic halo.

"It could be helpful if you untied my hands."

Lotus nodded, and Phil jerked the ropes off his wrists. When his hands were free, Jeffrey struggled to his feet and dug into one of his pockets. He pulled out a wrinkled white envelope.

"This is a marriage license," he said. "I brought it

hoping to convince Elizabeth to sign it. As you can see, I have already signed it. So has one witness, the matron of honor."

"Your sister?" Lotus asked.

"My mother. This was actually her idea."

Lotus raised his eyebrows. "What are you proposing?"

"I am proposing that Phillip here serve as best man and sign his name. And I am suggesting that Sirens, your crooked cop, sign as officiator. We hurried the wedding because I did not want to leave Elizabeth alone with her depression and without someone to hold her though those long, lonely nights. But unfortunately, the depression was too much for her."

"What happened after her untimely death?" Lotus asked.

"Her husband allowed a group of men to search his property for a potential treasure trove. He allowed this in exchange for a double share."

"Double?" Phil asked. "Why would we give you a double share?"

"One for myself and one for my mother. She has expensive medical needs that require attention."

"Why don't we just go to the courthouse and get another license?" Phil asked. "No one would believe that Elizabeth Hammond would marry this guy."

Jeffrey straightened himself. "In both the article about her son's disappearance and in the obituary, I was mistakenly referred to as her fiancé. That mistake was never corrected. Also, I had already proposed to Mrs. Hammond before her son's disappearance. Were he to return alive, he would be disappointed to find me to be his legal guardian, but he would not be surprised."

A loud thump came down the hall from the back bedroom. The thump multiplied and became thumping.

"Phil," Lotus said. "Go tell your attention-starved lady friend to quiet down."

Phil didn't move. "I don't like this," he said.

"Go now!" Lotus said, and glared at Phil. "Mr. Veatch, I will sign as your best man since I think Phil would rather not." Lotus lit a cigarette and began patting his pockets for a pen. "We can get things rolling this evening."

"Don't sign anything, Lotus," Phil said. "We should have a meeting!" But he was finally walking down the hall.

Elizabeth was confused. The first pop beneath her had made her wonder about the strength of the bed. She had actually felt the second pop. The bed had jostled slightly. Elizabeth rolled onto her side and arched so that she could look out the window behind her. What were they doing out there? Were they tearing her house apart now? The bed almost hopped beneath her.

Then it did hop, and she bounced toward the edge. She started to shift herself so that she wouldn't fall. The bed jumped. The posts shook. Good grief, what were they doing? Elizabeth braced herself to roll off, but she was near the edge now, and the next thump tipped her over. She landed on her face on the thin carpet, her arms still tied behind her.

The thumping continued. Her nose started to bleed. Elizabeth pulled her head up and tried to blink her watering eyes clear. Then came a crash. They had definitely broken something. It sounded like wood. She could hear Phil yelling something in the hall. There were other voices as well, the men outside. She put her head on the floor and waited.

Her door opened.

"Elizabeth, what are you trying to accomplish?" Phil asked.

"I fell," she said.

Phil looked around, then shut the door carefully behind him. He stepped over Elizabeth's body and crouched beside the bed.

"Listen to me, Elizabeth," he said. "Lotus just decided to marry you to Jeffrey. Not really, but they're going to fake it and then make it look like you killed yourself. Veatch gets the land and a share of the treasure. I'm your only chance right now. I can't stop them. Say you'll marry me, and I'll get you out of here.

I've got a gun. We could get out of here easy. We'll get the sheriff, round up all these jokers, and send 'em off to where they belong. The land will be ours, the treasure will be ours."

Elizabeth said nothing.

"Elizabeth," Phil said. "They killed your husband. They killed Ted. I heard them talking. Pook made it look like he died in a plane wreck, but they found him in the caves and killed him."

Elizabeth rolled up onto her side to look at him.

"What?" she asked.

"They killed Ted," Phil said. "And his friend too. He was there."

Elizabeth's mind began to whirl. What friend? Ted only had one friend. Reg? His father had said he was missing. Reg hadn't come to the funeral. He'd never answered his phone or any letters. That morning . . .

Her mind froze. The bed behind Phil was moving. No. It was opening. The tangled bedspread, the mattress, the tattered dust ruffle were all rising between the bedposts, rising on two filthy straining arms. A head appeared between them. A man's head encrusted with dust. Hair stuck out in all directions, and a thick beard was braided on his chest. His eyes were squinting against the daylight-filled room. A smaller head came up beside the first one. It looked at her.

"Mom?" it said. A dog squirted out.

❋   ❋   ❋

Phil spun around in surprise, tripped, and sat on Elizabeth. She would have yelled, but his weight knocked all the wind out of her lungs.

"Reg! Hurry. She's tied up." It was her son's voice. Was she dead already? Tom had been hiding under the bed? With Reg? That wasn't Reg. She heard grunting. Grunting on top of her and somewhere else. The weight was gone. Phil was standing again. She opened her eyes to see the bed slam shut. The room rocked with the sound.

The filthy man was standing up now. He was wearing a tiny shirt, and his eyes were still shut. Tom and a few inches of dirt stood beside him.

"Tom, I can't see," Reg said. "My eyes." Clean tear tracks were running down his face.

"Lotus!" Phil yelled. "Lotus!"

Lotus leaned against the doorjamb and held the screen door open.

"Can I help you?" he asked.

"I'm here to see Elizabeth," Nestor said, and gritted his teeth at the fat man.

"She's actually napping right now," Lotus said. "The doctor thought she needed some sleep."

"Hmm," Nestor said. "What are you doin' here while she's nappin'?"

Lotus chuckled. "Nothing improper. Some of us offered to help her find her son."

"You think he might be in the living room then?" Nestor leaned in across Lotus's arm. A haloed Jeffrey was staring at him from the couch. Sirens was in the kitchen. "What happened to him?" Nestor asked, and pointed at Jeffrey.

An enormous crash filled the house.

Lotus didn't flinch. "He slipped on some rocks. We brought him back here for treatment."

"Ah," Nestor said. "A plastic bag always does the trick."

"Lotus!" Phil's voice called. "Lotus!"

"I'll just come back some other time," Nestor said. "Maybe when things are less hectic." He smiled, turned, and walked back to the stairs. Lotus thanked him and shut both doors.

Tom tried to step toward his mother but was pushed back by the grinning man.

"Your mother's been worried about you, Tom," Phil said. "Come on out here. There are some people I want you to meet. People who've been helping look for you. You too, Reg. Elizabeth will be fine waiting here." Phil reached out and grabbed Reg by the shoulder. Reg shrugged his hand off.

"What's going on?" he asked. "Who's tied up?"

Phil laughed, made a fist, and slammed it into Reg's jaw. The blind man stumbled and then spread his length out on the floor. Tom lashed out at Phil. He punched at the man's face, and when his blows were brushed away, he kicked at his legs. Argus bit Phil in the calf as hard as he was able.

Phil yelped and kicked at the dog. He reached for the small of his back and brought around a black gun.

Reg, lying on the floor, tried to open his eyes. The light in the room was too much for them, weakened by three years of darkness and sputtering flame. They had been streaming tears even before Phil's blow. But Reg was unwilling to be blind in a fight. He forced his eyes open, as open as they would go. At first, there was nothing but burning and whiteness, and then, coming into focus slowly, there was a face. A face like this one had stood over him in a cave three years ago, a face young and smug and angry. And just like three years ago, he could see—a dragon wrapping a chest and shoulder and, below the shoulder, an arm extending. The arm held a gun. Reg gathered himself and lunged. The gun fired, and the top of Reg's head met Phil's chin. The two men tumbled to the ground, both straining.

Tom jumped to help Reg, but the gun went off again, and he could see Reg needed no help. He turned to his mother, but his eyes took in the body

of Argus. The first bullet had gone through his back-
bone. Gus's tongue was still lolling, and he was trying
to breathe.

Tom fell to the ground beside his mother and
began pulling at the rope that held her wrists.

"It's okay, Mom," he said. "It's okay. I think Reg
shot him."

"There's more," she said, and the door opened.
Lotus looked in.

"Phil?" he asked.

"Phil's dead." It was Reg. He had rolled off the body
and his eyes were shut again, but he was pointing the
gun at Lotus's voice. "I can shoot you too."

Lotus closed the door carefully and stepped back
into the hall.

"Sirens," he whispered. "Get up here." But Sirens
didn't come.

"Sirens," Lotus whispered again, and looked
around. The old man who had been at the door was
pointing a shotgun at him. His face was red and he was
out of breath. Sirens and Jeffrey were both lying on
their faces in the living room with their hands on their
heads. Nestor had said he would come back, and he
had. He'd had to get his shotgun out of the truck first.

"Name's Nestor," he said.

Lotus dove for the closest door. Nestor's shotgun
roared, and a cloud of rock salt, the very angriest kind

of bee, rattled and ricocheted around the end of the hall. Most of it found a home in Lotus's fat side.

"I almost wish it was buckshot," Nestor muttered. "Elizabeth?" he yelled. "You okay?"

"Nestor? Is that you?" The bedroom door opened, and Elizabeth's face peered down the hall. "I'm okay. Tom's here too. He's back, and Reg Fisher."

It only took a moment after things had settled for Elizabeth to start crying. She held Tom in her arms while Nestor called the sheriff to come pick up three men and a body. She even laughed when Pook tried to walk back into the house with Cy and the twins behind him. Nestor had been too slow that time. The four men had launched themselves down the stairs and off the enormous rock while angry clouds of salt rattled on the handrail behind them.

Elizabeth found Reg a pair of Ted's old aviator glasses, and the filthy man sat on the couch with tears rolling out from behind the mirror lenses, doing their best to wash his cheeks before they got lost in his beard. He held Argus's bloody body on his lap, had been holding him when his breathing stopped.

Tom cried too, but only because everyone else was. Nestor admired Reg's beard and then paced the rock until the valley was full of sirens and the house was crowded with deputies.

When that had happened, Nestor opened the door and led Tom, Elizabeth, and Reg out on the rock. There, while they stood and Reg wept at the wind and the sky, at every cloud and every creaking tree, Nestor spat on the rock and honored Argus, the best of all dogs.

And then they sat, Reg, Elizabeth, and Tom, with their legs dangling over the edge of the rock, and they couldn't decide if they should laugh or cry, and so they did both. Elizabeth gripped her son with arms that couldn't stop squeezing. She rubbed her face in the dirt of his hair and wiped her tears on his forehead. Tom squeezed his mother and lost the smell of death, of cold stone and water, in the scent of her skin.

For Reg, there was no end to sensation. Even through his glasses his eyes burned. His skin crawled in the warm breeze and sent up goose bumps to celebrate. Every breath, every smell, and the laughter of faraway insects, every bit of the world's dance greeted him at once, and the noise overwhelmed him. From the rippling green and the lazy willows beneath them to the blue kingdom and its cloud herds above, all the world rose up, stood on its head, and crushed his soul with joy.

~ fourteen ~

CRAZY BERRY

When the new refrigerator arrived, things had changed. Many stories had been told, and people all around had heard about the missing boy and the missing man who came out of the mountain into a hidden storm cellar beneath an old carved bed. But there was no talk of treasure, at least at first, and very little talk of going back in. Reg had shaved his beard, and Elizabeth had given him a haircut. While she did, she'd asked him a question.

"Just how much treasure do you think is down there?"

"Not as much as there is up here" was his answer. And he meant it.

Phil Leiodes was cremated, and his doting aunt—after seeing a late-night commercial—sent his ashes off to be turned into a yellow diamond. It came back smaller than she'd expected.

Jeffrey Veatch put his mother into Sunshine Acres Rest Home and then moved to a remote part of Mexico, where he immediately drank the water.

The deliverymen strained and sweated but survived. Elizabeth had them take the fridge box with them when they left, and Reg ran a water line to the dispenser in the door. That evening, Nestor arrived in clean overalls and brought all of his dogs with him.

A celebratory cookout was required, and the hectic business of coming back to life—hospital and doctor visits, interviews with journalists and authorities—could only put it off for so long. Elizabeth wouldn't allow cheap processed meat at her celebration, requiring instead, at a minimum, fat expensive sausages. Reg insisted on burning them. At least his. He wanted it black and wrinkly—as unlike boiled meat as he could make it.

A large RV was parked in the gravel at the base of the rock, and Reg's father and his friend Leonard from the Smithsonian stood around the grill asking Reg questions. They wanted to date the bed. They wanted to see how it opened and examine the storm cellar. They wanted to know when the house had been built and if the builders knew what they were hiding or just parked a house on ruins and called it a free cellar like so many other Europeans in the New World.

Sausages were a waste of time. They wanted to descend long stone steps into darkness.

Reg looked at their wide bodies and laughed. "You won't fit," he said. "But you'll get your chance. You'll sign papers first, strict limitations. I have to approve the removal of any items, and there are some I will not."

"Like what?" Leonard asked.

"The sarcophagus," Reg said. "He wanted to be there, let him be there."

"That's ridiculous," Leonard said. "This could've been done by Admiral Cheng. It could *be* Cheng. It could be Fu Hsi, the tamer of the animals. If this is the tomb of a mythical Asian character in the New World, I don't need to tell you that it would be the most substantial, the most epic find of this century. The whole history of North America could be rewritten."

"We'll let him lie," Reg's father said. "Perfectly understandable. But you realize that when word of this gets around, you won't be able to stop excavation. The land will be taken, the government will bring in archaeologists. Treasure laws are tight. You might get a finder's fee, but that's it."

"Treasure law doesn't apply, Dad. We found it in the basement. As for his stuff, well, I'll take a look someday, and you two can come with me when I do. There are only a couple things I want to bring out now."

When the evening ended, Reg stood beside Elizabeth, chewing on a final sausage. Her arm was around Tom's shoulders, and they were looking at the stars.

"Have you ever noticed how much the world is like a firework?" Reg asked.

"No," Elizabeth said. "Fireworks are always an anticlimax, they're depressing afterward. The world isn't like that."

"Hmm," Reg said. "Thomas, are you ready for our anticlimax?"

Tom nodded.

Reg went inside, and when he came back, he and Tom walked to the chain on the back corner of the house and began climbing. When they sat beside each other on the lip of the chimney, Reg handed Tom a small box.

"Crazy Berry, Tom?" Reg asked.

"Crazy Berry," Tom said. The two of them sat and drank their artificial flavoring through jointed straws.

"This isn't berry," Reg said. "It tastes like grape."

Tom laughed.

"It is crazy, though," Reg added. "I'll give it that."

When the box drinks would do nothing but burble and slurp, Reg grew serious.

"Thomas Hammond," he said. "There's a question I would like to ask your mother, but I want to ask you first."

If you have the good fortune of living near the valley where a small mountain peak once shaped like a crescent moon fell down and disturbed the willow trees that grow beside a slow stream, then you may have seen the old house chained to the top of the enormous rock, and you are sure to have heard of all the things that came out of its basement. There was the gold and the statues and the ancient armor and the stacks of cuneiform tablets that had molded so close together over the centuries that the first people who found them mistook them for thick pillars standing around a sarcophagus. Most of the treasures, at least those made public, are now in museums. But if you are curious enough, and you walk up the long stairs to the top of the rock, and you knock on the door, then it may be answered by a tall man with dark hair and bright eyes or by a pretty lady who is quick to laugh. You may even find yourself looking at a lean young man with a wide smile. And if you are brave enough to ask to see some of the treasure from the mountain, they will point you to the side of the rock that connects with the ridge. It is usually bright there, only shaded at sunset, and a flat spot has been cleared in the earth. This is where they keep the first treasure taken from the mountain.

There are three stones set up, and two of them have rough edges. The first says nothing more than ARGUS and is plain. The second has a simple cross and says THE OLD MAN WHO LEFT A LIGHT. The third has a cross and a roughly carved border. It says THEODORE DOLIUS HAMMOND. And underneath that is written IN THE GROUND, THE BEST SEED IS NEVER WASTED.

AUTHOR'S NOTE

Leepike Ridge does not draw inspiration from any historical evidence that proto-Chinese explorers reached the New World. Rather, it draws inspiration from a much broader pattern. Virtually everywhere on this planet that modern man (from the Age of Exploration on) has traveled, there have been people and cultures already rooted and waiting to be "discovered."

Civilizations rise and fall like tides. When other civilizations happen upon them, it can be difficult to tell whether they are at their height or have already fallen and are in decay. The New World was rich with tribes in every region when the Europeans arrived. Our Polynesian cousins had discovered, populated, and built a culture on their islands long before Europeans thought to look for them. Lewis and Clark walked across a mostly unknown continent and were never long without human contact. Stone-walled cities stand unexplained in Zimbabwe—discovered empty.

In the angriest deserts of Africa, in the bush of

Australia, on obscure Pacific islands, primitive man carved out life and held on to it. Some left only small tokens to mark their graves—signs that they had lived and died—while others left impossible ruins in the peaks of Peru.

Going where no man has gone before is more difficult than it sounds. Our cousins and ancestors were no less curious than we are, and were perhaps bolder. This world is their tomb.

You should look under the bed.

GRATITUDE

Homer for *The Odyssey*
Twain for Sawyer
Coldplay for Track Four
Joe C. for The First Voyage
Jim T. for The Pencil
Aaron for Leaptide
Mom and Dad for All the Milk
H.L.W.

Behind each door,
a startling secret . . .

Turn the page for a preview of
N. D. Wilson's inventive,
world-hopping
fantasy adventure.

CHAPTER ONE

Henry, Kansas, is a hot town. And a cold town. It is a town so still there are times when you can hear a fly trying to get through the window of the locked-up antique store on Main Street. Nobody remembers who owns the antique store, but if you press your face against the glass, like the fly, you'll see that whoever they are, they don't have much beyond a wide variety of wagon wheels. Yes, Henry is a still town. But there have been tornadoes on Main Street. If the wind blows, it's like it won't ever stop. Once it's stopped, there seems to be no hope of getting it started again.

There is a bus station in Henry, but it isn't on Main Street. It's one block north—the town fathers hadn't wanted all the additional traffic. The station lost one-third of its roof to a tornado fifteen years ago. In the same summer, a bottle rocket brought the gift of fire to its restrooms. The damage has never been repaired, but the town council makes sure that the building is painted fresh every other year, and always the color of a swimming pool. There is never graffiti. Vandals would have to drive more than twenty miles to buy the spray paint.

Every once in a long while, a bus creeps into town and eases to a stop beside the mostly roofed, bright aqua station with the charred bathrooms. Henry is always glad to see a bus. Such treats are rare.

On this day, the day our story begins, bus hopes were high. The Willis family was expecting their nephew, and the mister and missus stood on the curb waiting for his arrival.

Mrs. Willis couldn't hold nearly as still as the town. She was brimful of nervous energy and busily stepped on and off the curb as if she were waiting for the bus to take her off to another lifetime of grammar school and jump rope. She had planned to wear her best dress on principle—it was the sort of thing her mother would have done—but she had no idea which of her dresses was best, or how to begin the selection process. It was even possible that she didn't have a dress that was best.

So she had remained in her sweatpants and T-shirt. She had been canning in her kitchen and looked pleasant despite the faded teal of her pants. Her face was steam-ruddied and happy, and her brown hair, which had originally been pulled back into a ponytail, had struggled free. On this day, if you got close enough, as her nephew would when hugged, she smelled very strongly of peaches. She was of medium build in every direction, and she was called Dotty by her friends, Dots by her husband, and Mrs. Willis by everyone else.

People liked Dotty. They said she was interesting. They rarely did the same for her husband. They said Mr. Willis was thin, and they didn't just mean physically. They meant thin everywhere and every way. Dotty saw much more than thin, and she liked him. Frank Willis didn't seem to notice much of anything beyond that.

Mrs. Willis stopped her stepping and backed away from the curb. Something was shimmering on the highway. The bus was coming. She nudged Frank and pointed. He didn't seem to notice.

The Henry on the bus was not a town in Kansas. He was simply a twelve-year-old boy on a slow bus from Boston, waiting to meet an aunt and uncle he had not seen since the age of four. He was not looking forward to reuniting with Aunt Dotty and Uncle Frank. Not because he in any way disliked them, but because he had led a life that had taught him not to look forward to anything.

The bus stopped amid a shower of metallic grunts. Henry walked to the front, said goodbye to a talkative old woman, and stepped onto the curb into a lung-taste of diesel. The bus lurched off, the taste faded, and he found that he was being held tight by someone rather soft, though not large, and the smell of diesel had been replaced by peaches. His aunt held him back by the shoulders, her smile faded, and she became suddenly serious.

"We are both so sorry about your parents," she said. She was diligently eye-wrestling him. Henry couldn't quite look away. "But we are very happy you're going to be staying with us. Your cousins are all excited."

Someone patted Henry on the shoulder. He looked up.

"Yep," Uncle Frank said. He was watching the bus march out the other end of town. "The truck's over here," he added, and gestured with his head.

Uncle Frank carried Henry's duffel bag while Aunt Dotty escorted him to the truck, one arm tightly wrapped around his shoulder. It was an old truck. A few decades earlier, it may have been a Ford. Then it had been donated as a shop-class project to Henry High. Uncle Frank bought it at an end-of-the-year fundraiser. The paint was scum brown, the sort that normally hides at the bottom of a pond, attractive only to leeches and easily pleased frogs. The class had not been able to afford the bigger wheels they had dreamed of, so they had simply lifted the truck body as high as the instructor would allow. The overall effect was one of startling ricketiness. Henry's bag was thrown into the truck bed.

"Hop in," Uncle Frank said, and pointed in the back. "The tailgate doesn't drop, so just stand on the tire there and hoick yourself over. I'll boost you a bit."

Henry stood on the tire and teetered for a moment, trying to get one leg over the edge of the truck bed. Uncle Frank pushed him from behind, and he tumbled in onto his side.

Henry had never ridden in the back of a truck before, and he had always assumed it was illegal, though on the one trip his parents had taken him on, a tour of early Southwestern settlements, he had seen an entire truckload of field workers drive by. As he had been strapped into a car seat in the back of a Volvo at the time, he was extremely jealous. Only a few miles later, he had learned to his surprise that nine-year-old boys do not usually ride in car seats. A laughing school bus full of children taught him the lesson at a stoplight.

Henry perched himself on one of the truck's wheel wells and prepared for a spiritual experience. The engine fired its way into life, Frank forced reluctant metal gears together, and Henry slid off the wheel well into the truck bed as Henry, Kansas, swirled through his hair. They drove one block before the truck shifted its weight in the saddle and muscled around a right turn.

Henry slipped onto his back and spread-eagled so he wouldn't roll. Two blocks later, the truck bounced hard, and gravel rattled in the wheel wells like gunshots. Henry watched a rooster tail of dust climb into the sky behind the truck, and he tried to keep from banging his head every time the truck hopped a pothole. Eventually Uncle Frank stopped with a strong pull on the emergency brake, and Henry slid headfirst into the back of the cab. He picked himself carefully up onto all fours and peered at a pale blue house that he vaguely remembered. Aunt Dotty was grinning at him in the side mirror, pointing at the house and waving.

The house seemed big, and an even bigger barn hulked behind it. A mostly white cat sprawled in the yard, looking revolted by something or other. Old leaded-glass windows lined the first floor, a row of small windows the second, and one big, round window perched up in the eaves. On the front porch, below a long row of green-tarnished wind chimes, three girls stood staring at him.

Henry sat on the wood floor with his back to a wall. The three girls sat facing him, all cross-legged. They were in the attic. The whole room was open. The walls coved, and an old rail guarded the top of some very steep stairs. Henry was looking to his left, out the big, round window at the far end, trying to avoid staring at his cousins as much as they were staring at him. To Henry's right, at the other end of the attic, a pair of small doors led into a space that was no longer the attic closet and was now Henry's bedroom. Uncle Frank had apologized for the size and pointed out, before Aunt Dotty threw an elbow to his ribs, that if Henry's parents were never heard from again and Henry had to live with them always, they would go ahead and knock the wall down and expand his room a bit.

Henry had thanked him.

"I'm Anastasia," the smallest girl said.

"I know," said Henry. She was the youngest, small and wiry for a nine-year-old. And freckled. Her hair was brown, but Henry thought it looked like it wanted to be red.

"Then how come you didn't say 'Hello, Anastasia' right off? Were you just being rude?"

"Hush," the oldest girl said.

Anastasia wrinkled her lip. "If you knew I was Anastasia, then what are their names?"

Henry looked to the oldest girl. Her straight, nearly black hair hung loose past her shoulders. She smiled at him.

"Penny," Henry said. He turned to the third girl, who had thick brown curls and green eyes. "And Henrietta."

Henrietta was staring at him. Henry looked away. He suspected he had done something rather awful to Henrietta's cat on his last visit. Suddenly the memory appeared vividly in the foreground of his mind and danced an emphatic jig. He turned red and Anastasia started talking again.

"What's Penny *stand* for?" she asked, narrowing her eyes.

Penny smiled and pulled her crossed legs tighter. "It doesn't stand for anything, Anastasia."

"It stands for Penelope," Anastasia insisted. "Doesn't it, Henry?" Henry shrugged, but Anastasia wasn't looking at him. She was looking at Henrietta.

Henrietta ignored her.

"No," Penny said. "It's *short* for Penelope, it doesn't *stand* for it. Standing for something is when you just do initials."

Henry tried to catch Henrietta's eye. "Do they call you Henry?" he asked.

"Yes," Henrietta said. Henry watched her jaw clench. "I don't like it," she added.

"Henrietta's too long," Anastasia said.

Henry thought for a moment. "It's no longer than Anastasia." He double-checked the syllables in his head. "Yeah."

"For a while I wanted to be called Josephine, but

then they just called me Jo." Henrietta looked at Henry. "Will you call me Beatrice?"

"Um, sure," Henry said.

"We'll call you Beat," Anastasia said, smiling.

"No, you won't," Henrietta said. "Not if you want to keep your teeth."

"Stop it," Penny said. "Why don't we just call you Henrietta? Now that *he's* here, we can't call you Henry."

Henrietta considered this option. She looked at Henry. She seemed to want him to agree.

"Okay," Henry said. They were silent again, and Henry's thoughts wandered back through his tour of the house.

The revolted cat—one of the girls had called him Blake—had quickly disappeared while Aunt Dotty led Henry onto the porch and very helpfully said, "Henry, you remember the girls."

Henry had then been attached to a human train, one back from the engine, on a high-speed tour of the house. He had seen sofas, gifts from dead great-aunts, lamps that didn't work, treasures acquired by Uncle Frank on the Internet (including a fish fossil now being used, uniquely and quite cheaply, Dotty pointed out, as an end table). Fingers pointed down the stairs into a dark basement. Various artistic pieces were highlighted, all produced by Frank and the girls. Aunt

Dotty had laughed and called them "especially local artists." Henry was shown the junk drawer, containing a small flashlight, a box of rubber bands, and a sedimentary layer of pens, pencils, paper clips, glue, and a plastic box with a picture of the ocean on its lid. He had seen the toilet, been shown the plunger, and heard of the plumbing trouble. He had been told to hold still and listen to see if the fridge would make its funny noise. It hadn't, but he had been warned that he would know when it did. And on the big second-story landing, there had been the door to the room at the front of the house. Henrietta had called it Grandfather's room, but no one had gone near it. Every other door in the house, every cabinet, every drawer, and every cupboard, had all been opened. But not that one.

Henry's mind snapped back. He was still on the floor in the attic. The girls had not yet grown weary of him and departed.

"Henry?" Anastasia said. "Henry, do you think your parents are going to die?"

Penny shot an eye-rebuke in her sister's direction, but it went unheeded. Henrietta and Anastasia were staring at Henry. Henrietta began twisting her hair.

Anastasia leaned forward. "Zeke Johnson's dad got killed by a combine."

"Stop it!" Penelope said. "If you don't want to talk about it, Henry . . ."

"Penelope likes Zeke," Anastasia said. Henrietta laughed.

Penelope darkened. "Everyone likes Zeke," she said.

Anastasia looked right into Henry's eyes. "He goes up to the graveyard by himself," she said. "And he pitches baseballs at his dad's gravestone."

Penelope crossed her arms. "Mr. Simon told him to write his dad a goodbye letter and he didn't want to. So he pitched to him instead."

"I don't want to talk about Zeke," Henrietta said. "Penny always talks about Zeke. I want to hear about Uncle Phil and Aunt Ursula."

"Do you think they're going to die?" Anastasia asked again.

Penelope sniffed. "You don't have to, Henry."

Henry pulled in a deep breath and then sighed. "No, it's okay. I don't know much, anyway. They got taken hostage riding their bicycles in Colombia. The men who talked to me at school said they would be ransomed back."

"What were they doing?" Henrietta asked.

"They're travel writers, and they wanted to write a book about bicycling across South America. They've been doing stuff like that ever since I was old enough to go to school."

"You've been to a lot of places, then," Henrietta said.

"No," Henry said. "They never take me with them. I've been to Disney World, but that was with a nanny. And California once."

Anastasia leaned forward. "Your parents really got kidnapped?" she asked. Henry nodded. "By guys with guns? Do you think they had masks? Your parents might be tied up in a cave somewhere right now."

"I don't know. Something like that," Henry said. "They got kidnapped, anyway."

The three girls were impressed, and they sat, chewing on lips or nails, examining Henry and quietly contemplating the situation.

After a moment, Frank's voice climbed loudly up the stairs. "Scrub the bones!" he yelled, and the attic echoed.

"What?" Henry asked.

The girls picked themselves up off the floor.

"Teeth," Henrietta said. "Brush your teeth."